Hardback - ISBN: 978-1-923567-30-6
Paperback - ISBN: 978-1-923567-31-3
eBook - ISBN: 978-1-923567-32-0

Cover design by **Holly Symons**
First Edition

For More, Please Visit

HollySymons.com.au

The Enchanted Goat of Buttermunch

A Norse Fairytale Retelling With Extra Beard Oil and
Goat Drool

A Rewrite Realms Spinoff Novella

(Prequel to Aurelya in Wonderrealm)

By HOLLY SYMONS

Sponsored Content (Totally Real Ads)

SPONSORED CONTENT

(Totally Real Ads)

GOATFLIX & CHILL

FIRE LOGS

GOAT-PROOF SCROLL COVERS

- **RESISTS DROOL**
- **PREVENTS CHEWING**
- **GUARANTEES SANITY**

PROTECT YOUR SCROLLS, AND YOUR SANITY!

BUTTERMUNCH'S
BEARD BUTTER
FOR BEASTS
TAME THE SCRUFF
A SPLENDID GROOMING BALM—
INFUSED WITH CEDARWOOD,
ROSEMARY, AND MAGIC!

Table of Contents

The Enchanted Goat of Buttermunch

A Norse Fairytale Retelling with Extra Beard Oil and Goat Drool

Book Two: The Goatfather's Grand Tour

A Realmsverse Cruise of Unparalleled Questionability

Book One: The Enchanted Goat of Buttermunch

A Norse Fairytale Retelling With Extra Beard Oil and Goat Drool

Prologue
In Which a Goat is Slightly Too Magical for Comfort

Let us begin, as all serious Norse histories do, with an *apology*.

You see, this tale, the one you are about to read, should have been carved into the sacred stones of history long ago, nestled between Odin's tree-hanging drama and Loki's... well, everything. But alas, it was *accidentally removed* from the mythological archives due to what scholars now refer to as "The Drool Incident."

At precisely 2:47 p.m. on an otherwise forgettable Tuesday in the Ninth Realm Archives, a goat enchanted, ambitious, and slightly too magical for anyone's comfort wandered into the scroll preservation chamber. What happened next is best described as an "aggressive nuzzle," followed by the consumption of seventeen critical scrolls, two library cards, and a small wax statue of Thor in a compromising pose.

The goat's name?

Sir Buttermunch.

Yes, that Buttermunch. The infamous, the bearded, the negotiator of three peace treaties and a particularly messy divorce between two frost giants. His legend was *supposed* to be taught in schools, whispered around campfires, and printed on goat-themed merchandise. Instead, it was lost beneath soggy parchment, faint goat hoofprints, and a baffled archivist named Knut.

For centuries, his story lived only in fragmented footnotes and obscure tavern songs ("The Ballad of the Hoofed Hustler," banned in four realms for reasons of decency). But no longer.

This is the official, completely accurate, somewhat chewed-around-the-edges tale of how Buttermunch the Goat outwitted kings, out-charmed princesses, and quite possibly negotiated himself a small kingdom using only a scroll, a seductive bleat, and an aggressive beard flip.

We advise you to proceed with caution, laughter, and possibly a napkin. There will be goat drool.

Chapter One
The Farm Boy, the Goat, and the Bread That Bit Back

Grimbold did not consider himself a brave man.
Nor a clever man.
Nor a man particularly skilled in the art of goat-wrangling, property negotiations, or defending himself from baked goods.

But fate, which has a cruel sense of humour and a soft spot for shaggy hooved creatures, had other plans.

It all began on a foggy morning when the air smelled faintly of dew, destiny, and something yeasty.
Grimbold, humble potato farmer of the Mud spout Hollow, was chasing his runaway turnip cart when he stumbled quite literally upon a goat.

Not just any goat.
The Goat.
Curled in the middle of the road like a misunderstood poem, with fur the colour of roasted chestnuts and an expression that suggested he'd once sued a frost giant and *won*.

"Are you injured?" Grimbold asked, blinking the mud out of his eyes.

The goat turned his head slowly majestically and replied, "Only my pride. And my mead supply. Also, my accommodations are frankly appalling."

Grimbold blinked again. "You… you talk?"

"Don't be ridiculous," said the goat. "I *converse*. There's a difference."

Grimbold, having had exactly zero hours of education in enchanted livestock etiquette, did what any sensible farm boy would do.

He offered the goat a slice of fresh bread.

The bread, enchanted by a traveling wizard who mistook it for his sentient sourdough starter, immediately leapt from Grimbold's hand and bit the goat on the ear.

The goat, unflinching, nodded solemnly. "A test. I respect that."

He then headbutted the bread into orbit and turned to Grimbold with regal authority.

"I am Sir Buttermunch, Third of That Name, Binder of Pacts, Devourer of Scrolls, and I hereby accept your service as my mortal sidekick. In return, I demand shelter, three gold horns of mead, and full ownership of the moon."

"The moon?" Grimbold whispered, already questioning his life choices.

"I'm flexible," said Buttermunch. "I'll settle for a small kingdom, a bath, and control over the local cheese economy."

And thus, without any real say in the matter, Grimbold the potato farmer became the reluctant companion to a goat with ambition, charisma, and a mild cheese addiction.

Little did he know, he had just enlisted in a quest that would rewrite the Realms, unseat a king, and require at least one dramatic monologue delivered atop a chandelier.

But first, mead.

Chapter Two
Sir Buttermunch Declares Himself a Knight, Lawyer, and Real Estate Agent

It is a well-known fact across most of the Realms that goats are not permitted to hold professional titles. This, however, has never stopped a goat from trying.

Especially *this* goat.

"I've thought it over," said Sir Buttermunch the following morning, his beard glistening with freshly applied butter oil. "And I've decided I shall now be addressed as *Sir Buttermunch, KLLRA. * That's Knight, Lawyer, and Licensed Real Estate Agent."

Grimbold blinked. "You're licensed?"

"Absolutely not," said Buttermunch proudly. "But I have a clipboard and *deep confidence issue, * which is basically the same thing."

They were halfway to the nearest village Swindlebrook when Buttermunch trotted into the local market square, announced his title to a stunned crowd, and immediately began correcting land boundaries using a stick, a map he found in a sandwich, and something he called "*Advanced Bleating Rhetoric. *"

The merchant objected.

Buttermunch responded by tap-dancing aggressively on a cabbage cart and reciting an obscure bylaw from the Treaty of Grumblethorpe.

The merchant attempted to bribe him with cheese.

Buttermunch accepted it, then fined him for "attempted bribery of an unlicensed goat officer."

Grimbold tried to intervene. "Maybe we should"

"No," said Buttermunch, without looking back. "Justice is grazing."

By noon, he had:
- Sold a condemned chicken shed as a "historic fixer-upper with ancient straw charm,"
- Represented a sheep in small-claims court (the plaintiff was a duck),
- And declared eminent domain over a garden gnome display.

The townsfolk, bewildered but too confused to argue, began referring to him as *The Hoofed Authority. * Children asked for autographs. One elderly woman tried to marry him.

And then came the *minor duke*.

Duke Strembling of Swindlebrook, a man with three monocles and zero patience, descended upon the scene with his guards and a voice like someone gargling pennies.

"What is the meaning of this?" he barked.

Buttermunch turned slowly, dramatically, and said, "Article 47b of the Realm Civic Charter permits legal reclamation of land if the agent involved possesses *either* a document of authority *or* exceptionally majestic facial hair."

Grimbold choked. "That can't be real!"

Buttermunch winked. "Neither is the Charter."

And just as the duke began to argue, **Odin's inspection guard** rode in likely following reports of goat-based zoning violations.

Buttermunch did not blink.

Instead, he threw down a hoof-drawn contract that claimed the village had already been reassigned as an *experimental grazing district under Royal Goat Oversight. *

"And where is your signature of approval?" demanded the guard.

Buttermunch grinned. "Right here," he said, and **stomped his hoof directly onto the parchment** with ceremonial flair. "Witnessed by mud. Sealed by hoof. Filed under destiny."

The guard paused, visibly unsure. "Well… the hoofprint is oddly official."

"Of course it is," Buttermunch said. "I used calligraphy mud."

That afternoon, Buttermunch was knighted by a bard with a stick, self-certified in real estate law using a mirror, and declared a local hero by a crowd that definitely wasn't sure what had just happened.

Grimbold watched it all unfold with the blank expression of someone experiencing an out-of-body moment between disbelief and mild indigestion.

He'd ask questions later. For now, he simply followed the goat.

And Buttermunch?

He trotted into the sunset, clipboard in mouth, head high, muttering legal jargon with flair.

Chapter Three
Odin, the Throne, and the Goat Who Negotiated a Treaty with a Tree

Odin, Allfather of the Realms, King of Asgard, Wearer of Dramatic Cloaks, had arrived.

He did not arrive quietly. Odin never arrived quietly. He arrived with thunder, lightning, and an eight-legged horse that refused to park properly.

"I sense… *unauthorised goat activity, *" Odin growled, dismounting with unnecessary flourish. "And possibly a zoning violation."

"Welcome to Swindlebrook," Buttermunch said, lounging in a hammock made of legal scrolls and turnip sacks. "Would you like to purchase a timeshare?"

Odin blinked once. Slowly. "No."

"Pity," said Buttermunch. "It comes with a view of the imaginary fjord and a complementary basket of cheese feelings."

Odin, not accustomed to being mocked by livestock, pointed his staff at the goat. "You. Goat. Explain yourself. Immediately."

Buttermunch stood, shook out his mane like a shampoo commercial, and began a PowerPoint presentation on a scroll. It unfurled dramatically, rolled into a puddle, and was promptly eaten by a passing duck.

"That was my only copy," said Buttermunch. "Fortunately, I've memorised it in interpretive bleating."

Grimbold groaned. "Oh no. Not again."

What followed was twenty-three minutes of hoof choreography, legal jargon, and increasingly elaborate metaphors involving acorns, beard rights, and a talking fence post named Gerald.

By the end of it, Odin was nodding solemnly and had accidentally signed over temporary royal authority to a tree.

The tree, newly sentient and alarmingly smug, renamed itself *King Barktholomew the Leafy* and immediately began demanding acorn taxes.

"What just happened?" Odin asked, blinking.

"You just lost jurisdiction over this hill," Buttermunch replied cheerfully. "And also, your backup throne."

"My *what*?"

"You brought a portable throne. It's right there," Buttermunch said, gesturing toward a folding chair with gold glitter and a "#1 Realm Dad" decal.

"I don't remember that."

"No one ever does," Buttermunch said gently.

Odin rubbed his temples. "Fine. I've been tricked. *Again. * You win this round, Goat."

"I win *every* round," Buttermunch said. "Even the ones I'm not invited to."

"And another thing!" Odin snapped, trying to recover some dignity. "I am hereby declaring goat drool a Class 4 Magical Biohazard!"

Buttermunch smirked. "Too late. I already bottled it."

"You WHAT?"

"It's called 'Essence of Authority.' Smells like confidence and aged cheese."

Grimbold handed Odin a tiny sample vial. Odin sniffed it. Immediately forgot why he was angry.

"Hmm," Odin muttered. "Smells like victory. And also regret."

"That's the top note," Buttermunch said. "The base note is lost paperwork."

By the time Odin left, trailing scroll crumbs and vague confusion, Buttermunch had secured three new titles, one small plot of land, and the official title of Honorary Woodland Ambassador to Sentient Trees.

He celebrated by headbutting a celebratory fruit basket and adding "Diplomat" to his growing list of jobs.

Grimbold, who had entirely stopped trying to understand anything, simply sighed.

And the tree?
Still king.

Chapter Four
The Castle, the Princess, and the Puffin That Wouldn't Die

The Castle of Fernsnort stood proudly on the edge of a cliff, daring gravity to object. It had towers, ramparts, and a drawbridge that squeaked like an offended duck.

Inside the castle lived Princess Fizzlefrond, heir to the realm, master of sighs, and owner of the largest collection of passive-aggressive teacups in the Nine Realms.

She was being held captive.
Voluntarily.

"I'm not technically imprisoned," she explained to her handmaidens. "I just find that hiding in a tower keeps expectations low and interruptions minimal."

This changed, of course, when a goat declared war on the puffin.

Sir Buttermunch had arrived.

Cloaked in a curtain he found behind a tavern and flanked by Grimbold (who still hadn't processed

Chapter Two), Buttermunch marched toward the castle gates with the confidence of a goat who had never lost an argument, even with a wall.

"Halt," said the guard. "State your business."

"I'm here to defeat the beast and claim the tower," said Buttermunch.

"What beast?"

"The enchanted puffin," Buttermunch whispered, eyes narrowing. "It's real. And it's personal."

The guard blinked. "We have… a puffin. It pecks at windows."

"It also cursed an orphan, insulted a shrub, and once threw a muffin at me during a legal summit."

"Are you sure it wasn't just a bird?"

"No one *is* sure," Buttermunch said darkly. "That's how it wins."

In the courtyard stood the puffin.

Small. Round. Eyebrows too judgmental for its size.

It stared at Buttermunch.
Buttermunch stared back.

A leaf fell. Tension mounted.

And then battle.

The puffin flapped. Buttermunch leapt sideways, hooves spinning like destiny in tap shoes.

The puffin squawked and charged. Buttermunch dodged and retaliated with a hoof-stomp distraction followed by aggressive bleating. The crowd gasped. Someone fainted. The puffin squawked again and puffed itself up to twice its size.

Grimbold screamed. "It's evolving!"

Princess Fizzlefrond arrived mid-squabble, assessed the chaos, and sighed so dramatically the flags wilted.

"Oh, for stars' sake," she muttered, marching into the arena. "Do I have to fix everything?"

She walked between them, plucked the puffin off the ground, stared it directly in its furious round eyes, and said, "No."

The puffin paused. Shrieked. Exploded into glitter. No one knew why.

"Well done," Buttermunch declared, brushing glitter from his beard. "We fought bravely."

"You headbutted a shrub and blamed it for your tactical misstep," Princess Fizzlefrond replied.

"Strategy," said Buttermunch. "Shrubs are suspicious."

"You're all ridiculous," she said. "And if I don't join you, I'll just end up ruling this place, and frankly I'm not in the mood for policy."

And just like that, Princess Fizzlefrond joined the quest.

"Grimbold," she said, eyeing the stunned farm boy. "Are you this confused all the time?"

"I yes," he said. "But I'm getting used to it."

"Good," she said. "You'll need that."

And so, the party grew: one goat, one reluctant potato boy, and one overqualified royal. The castle gates opened. The townsfolk cheered. The shrub recovered.

But somewhere... deep in the forest...
A puffin reassembled.

The war was not over.

Chapter Five
Chad's Glittery Manifestation Retreat (With Bonus Goat Yoga)

Deep in the Fernsnort Woods, where logic dared not tread and mushrooms wore monocles, there lived a goblin.

His name was Chad.

He was not, technically, qualified in anything.
Except vibes.

With a velvet robe two sizes too long, a pouch of "emergency glitter," and a staff made entirely of recycled affirmation scrolls, Chad had transformed a clearing into a self-declared wellness retreat called:

"Chad's Glittery Manifestation Retreat & Magical Soul Awakening Spa Hut (Now with Goat Yoga)."

He had one star on Realm Advisor. He gave it to himself.

Buttermunch led the group into the clearing with purpose.

"I booked us a team-building session," he announced. "Our party lacks cohesion, snacks, and core flexibility."

Fizzlefrond looked around. "This feels like a scam."

"It is," said Chad, emerging from a puff of glitter. "But it's a motivated scam."

He bowed, lost his balance, and landed in a pile of positivity pamphlets titled Manifesting Moisturised Outcomes.

Grimbold opened one. "This says my 'inner fruit' is overripe."

"You are looking a little dehydrated," Chad said gently. "Would you like a chaos smoothie?"

"What's in it?"

"Unclear."

The retreat began with a guided intention howl (mostly Chad yelling "I AM A SACRED PINECONE" at a cloud), followed by Goat Yoga, which involved Buttermunch standing on everyone's backs until enlightenment was achieved or bones popped.

Then came the acorn-throwing incident.

Loki's Squirrel had followed the party, fuelled by jealousy, caffeine, and unresolved rodent angst. It perched on a branch above the retreat, glaring down at Buttermunch with tiny vengeful eyes.

When Chad attempted a demonstration of "spiritual stillness," the squirrel launched a barrage of acorns with sniper-like precision.

Thwack.
"My ENERGY CENTERS!" Chad cried, toppling into his smoothie vat.

Buttermunch leapt onto a rock, shouted "I DECLARE US UNDER NUT-BASED SIEGE!" and began counter-bleating.

Princess Fizzlefrond did not assist. She was too busy laughing behind a tree.

Grimbold was hit six times and passed out mid-meditation. He awoke believing he was a sentient muffin.

After the third round of goat yoga and one "healing glitter explosion," Chad handed everyone handwritten manifestation scripts ("You are powerful. You are capable. You are 73% moisture.")

"Remember," Chad said, dripping smoothie from his ears, "if your aura gets tangled, just do interpretive goblin squats and yell your fears at a decorative rock."

Buttermunch nodded solemnly. "We'll do that. Daily."

Chad winked. "Your goat is spiritually advanced."

"He's also legally a lawyer now," Grimbold muttered.

"I rest my case," Chad said, and vanished in a puff of lavender mist.

As the group walked away, slightly stickier and emotionally confused, Buttermunch pulled out his glitter-splattered clipboard.

"Well, that was deeply unhelpful. But now we're aligned," he said.

"With what?" Fizzlefrond asked.

"No clue," said Buttermunch. "But my chakras are vibrating, and I think one of them is trying to unionise."

Somewhere behind them, a squirrel screeched, an acorn exploded, and a cloud of glitter erupted into the sky.

The quest continued.

Chapter Six
The Wedding, The Coronation, and the Hoofprint in History

It began, as most great Realmsverse disasters do, with a brunch invitation and a questionable prophecy.

Princess Fizzlefrond had agreed to marry Buttermunch.

Not out of love.
Not even out of strategy.
But because she found the idea funny and was curious to see if the vows included tax deductions.

"I mean, he's already declared himself King of Legal Gray Areas," she said. "We may as well throw in a tiara."

Grimbold, by now emotionally detached from logic, was in charge of flower arrangements. He decorated the aisle with turnips. No one stopped him.

The wedding was held in a meadow legally renamed "Buttermunchia" following a clerical error involving three ducks and a corrupted spreadsheet.

Guests included:
- Chad (officiating with a crystal wand he won in a raffle),
- A sentient shrubbery quartet performing the anthem "Goat You To The Moon,"
- The Squirrel (invited by accident, currently disguised as a cake).

"Do you, Sir Buttermunch, take this very confused princess to be your co-ruler, lunch partner, and co-signer on enchanted property deeds?" Chad asked solemnly.

"I do," said Buttermunch, presenting a legally binding scroll titled "Marriage License & Tax-Exempt Alliance Form 17b."

"And do you, Fizzlefrond, take this goat to be your royal headache and designated beard fluffer?"

Fizzlefrond sighed. "Sure. Why not."

Chad threw glitter. Someone sneezed sparkles.

Immediately after the vows, a coronation ceremony began.

Buttermunch, crowned with a salad bowl he declared "symbolic," took the throne (a stack of real estate brochures) and announced:

"As my first act as goat-king, I hereby pardon all bread-related crimes and declare Wednesdays free of logic!"

The crowd cheered. Mostly because they were paid in snacks.

Then Grimbold tripped over a ceremonial candle and accidentally summoned something.

A portal opened. Wind roared. Dramatic music played from nowhere.

Out stepped…
King Puffin, Reassembled and Reenchanted.
He wore a tiny crown. His eyebrows glowed.

"YOU," the puffin bellowed. "MARRIED THE PRINCESS AND CLAIMED THE THRONE?"

Buttermunch stood proudly. "Yes. And also, the cheese rights."

The puffin screeched, summoned a lightning fork, and flapped furiously toward the altar.

Grimbold panicked and threw a turnip. It bounced off the puffin's beak.

"YOU'VE MADE A POWERFUL ENEMY," the puffin growled.

"And a slightly flustered husband," Fizzlefrond added.

There was chaos.
There was yelling.
Chad tried to meditate through it. The Squirrel bit someone. The shrubbery quartet caught fire briefly.

Buttermunch, ever the professional, stomped a contract onto the puffin's wing and shouted, "I COUNTER-CLAIM YOUR INVASION WITH CLAUSE 32: NO TAKE-BACKSIES."

The puffin blinked. "That's not real law."

"It is now," Buttermunch replied. "I hoofnotarised it."

And just like that, the puffin vanished. Again. Probably to return in a later chapter.

The coronation concluded in a flurry of cake, confetti, and legal confusion. A statue was unveiled featuring Buttermunch mid-bleat with the inscription:

"HERE STOOD THE GOAT WHO RUINED EVERYTHING AND MADE IT BETTER."

Grimbold looked around at the ruined meadow, the glitter in his eyebrows, the goat crown, the legally binding puffin clause, and said softly:

"...This is somehow the least weird day we've had."

And so, it ended.

The wedding was real.
The coronation was maybe real.
The puffin was possibly immortal.
And Buttermunch, for all his bleats and scrolls, had
left a hoofprint on history so dramatic that the
Realmsverse would never be the same.

But don't worry.
There's absolutely no way any of this could go wrong
in the sequel.

...Right?

Chapter Seven
The Tax Collector, the Turnip War, and the Goat Who Refused to Declare Income

It was a quiet morning in Buttermunchia, which was suspicious in itself.

Birds chirped. Grimbold was attempting to balance teacups on his head for "spinal awareness." Princess Fizzlefrond was editing their group crest to include fewer cheese wedges.

Then a trumpet blared. Loudly. And also in C minor, which made it especially threatening.

A cart rolled up to the castle gates. Upon it sat a small, angular man in a green waistcoat that screamed "auditorial menace." His scrolls were neatly stacked. His glasses glinted. His name tag read:

Derek, Realm Revenue Enforcement Division – Tier IV

"OH NO," Buttermunch gasped, ducking behind a decorative shrub.

"Who is *that*?" asked Fizzlefrond.

"*The taxman, *" Buttermunch whispered. "He's here for the Annual Declarations of Unofficial Royal Revenue. We didn't file."

"You haven't earned any revenue," Grimbold said.

"That's not the point," Buttermunch snapped. "I've committed to the aesthetic of wealth. That counts."

Derek stepped forward, unfurled a scroll, and read aloud in the most emotionless monotone the Realms had ever endured:

"You are hereby summoned to declare all financial gains, enchanted trade deals, mystical item acquisitions, and suspiciously gifted wheels of cheese dating back to… the puffin incident."

"Objection!" Buttermunch yelled.

"This isn't court."

"Well, it should be!"

They were fined immediately for shouting.

So began the Turnip Audit War.

To avoid further declarations, Buttermunch invoked an obscure farming clause "if taxation occurs during harvest, the taxed may defend their assets via produce warfare."

"It's real," he claimed.

"It's ridiculous," Derek said.

"Still counts," Fizzlefrond sighed, tossing Buttermunch a ceremonial pitchfork.

Turnips flew. Declarations were ducked. Chad appeared halfway through with a smoothie for "financial alignment."

Grimbold was briefly promoted to Comptroller of Root Vegetables, a title revoked minutes later after he tried to tax the moon.

Derek, armed with nothing but his stamp of disapproval, pressed on.

Buttermunch countered with a tactical double-bleat feint, a signed scroll declaring Buttermunchia a "Temporary Fiscal Mirage Zone," and an interpretive tax dance.

The Realmsverse Ministry of Paperwork exploded trying to process it.

In the end, they reached a diplomatic compromise.

Buttermunch agreed to pay one enchanted coin, one soggy receipt, and a goat-drawn doodle of "future projected income" labelled *Maybe Profits? *

Derek accepted it with a sigh, handed over a business card that turned into a mushroom, and left without making eye contact.

"You do realise," Fizzlefrond said, "we just won a war against taxation using vegetables and a goat tantrum."

"I know," Buttermunch said proudly. "I'm going to add 'Treasurer' to my titles."

Grimbold groaned. Chad floated by on a glitter cloud, muttering something about "emotional refunds."

And in a dusty vault beneath the Realms, the puffin… took note.

"Soon," he whispered. "Very soon."

Chapter Eight
The Puffin's Revenge (And the Great Squirrel Sabotage)

There was a chill in the air.

Not the usual kind, the mystical kind. The kind that smells faintly of vengeance, puffin feathers, and unresolved legal action.

Grimbold felt it first.

He shivered while buttering toast. "Does anyone else feel like they're being watched by something… flightless but emotionally intense?"

Fizzlefrond raised an eyebrow. "The Puffin?"

"Worse," Buttermunch said, emerging from a pile of scrolls with wild eyes. "The Puffin… with paperwork."

It arrived on a ceremonial wind. A golden scroll with glowing ink slammed into the breakfast table, knocking over Chad's smoothie and launching a turnip into orbit.

The scroll unfurled itself and read aloud in an aggressively pompous voice:

"To the so-called 'Realm of Buttermunchia,'
From His Feathery Highness King Puffin the
Reassembled,
You are hereby summoned to attend a mandatory
Realm-wide Mediation Summit™ to address your
unlawful crown claim, emotional damages, and one
(1) stolen enchanted breadstick."

"I didn't steal it," Buttermunch hissed. "It was a
diplomatic snack!"

Meanwhile… in the Trees

The Squirrel had returned.

And this time, it had plans.

Perched in a camouflaged hammock made of stolen
shoelaces and passive-aggressive post-it notes, the
Squirrel activated its acorn comms network.

It contacted King Puffin using a squeaky pinecone
communicator.

"I'm in," the Squirrel whispered. "Operation Winged
Fury is go."

"Good," the Puffin squawked. "Initiate chaos. Target
the goat."

Back in Buttermunchia, things escalated quickly.

Fizzlefrond was preparing rebuttal speeches. Chad was crafting a defence spell out of essential oils and confusing metaphors. Grimbold was trying to wear a tie and failing dramatically.

Buttermunch?
He declared Trial by Interpretive Dance.

The Summit Begins

The Realms-wide Mediation Summit was held in the Grand Neutral Meadow, beneath a banner reading:

"Welcome Litigants! Please Leave Your Weapons and Passive-Aggression at the Door."

Representatives arrived:
- King Puffin with a lawyer owl named Gregory,
- A delegation of confused turnip farmers,
- And the Squirrel, disguised as a juice vendor with evil in its tiny eyes.

Buttermunch took the stage in a sequined cape and began his defence: a twenty-minute interpretive dance called "The Bleat of Truth."

It involved:
- Goat yoga,
- Dramatic lunges,
- And one midair leap that knocked out Gregory the lawyer owl.

King Puffin was unimpressed.

"Enough of this nonsense!" he bellowed. "This goat has mocked my reign, stolen my bakery rights, and declared war on my eyebrows!"

"Technically," Buttermunch said mid-split, "I only declared war on your attitude."

That's when the Squirrel struck.

Acorns rained down like tiny nutty meteors. Chad was hit in the chakra. Grimbold screamed something about jam. Fizzlefrond pulled a sword out of her handbag.

"DEFEND THE DANCE," Buttermunch shouted, spinning like an aggressive cheese wheel.

In the end, no one won the trial. The puffin stormed off. The Squirrel was arrested by the shrubbery guards (again). And the meadow caught fire from Chad's manifestation candles.

A final ruling was scribbled on a napkin and said simply:

"This feels like a later problem. – Realms Court"

Back home, covered in glitter and confusion, Grimbold asked, "Are we still being sued?"

"Yes," Buttermunch said. "But spiritually? I feel acquitted."

Fizzlefrond groaned. Chad offered everyone smoothies. They declined.

And far away... in a puffin-sized fortress carved into a cliff...

A puffin army began to march.

Chapter Nine
The Secret Council of Slightly Off-Brand Wizards

According to absolutely no official Realmsverse records (and a suspicious napkin map Chad kept in his sock), deep beneath the Goblin Hills existed a hidden society known only as:

"The Secret Council of Slightly Off-Brand Wizards."

They were not licensed.
They were not respected.
They were, however, fabulously dramatic.

Which is why Buttermunch had to join immediately.

The Entrance Exam (Also a Cheese Tasting)

The entrance was hidden behind a waterfall shaped like a disappointed goose. To gain access, Buttermunch had to answer a riddle while blindfolded and wearing socks soaked in glitter tonic.

The riddle?
"What walks on hooves, speaks in bleats, and claims to be a certified tax lawyer?"

"Buttermunch," he answered. "Also, possibly Chad if he's possessed again."

The waterfall split open with a sparkly whoosh. The goat had passed.

Inside, a spiral staircase made of semi-sentient books led to a chamber filled with mystical fog, floating furniture, and one suspiciously quiet baguette wearing a monocle.

Buttermunch bowed respectfully.
The baguette said nothing. It was, after all, a baguette.

No one questioned it.

The Council

The council consisted of seven slightly unstable, fabulously dressed former students of the Academy of Arcane Alignment™ who had all been expelled for "excessive flair and spontaneous glitter explosions."

They introduced themselves as:
1. Rhyma the Rhymer – Spoke only in couplets.
Dramatic, moody, allergic to logic.
2. Flambouros the Loud – Wore a hat that screamed.
3. Mistress Featherella – Constantly surrounded by swirling birds and unverified prophecies.
4. Gregory (The Wizard Formerly Known as Susan) – Had a goat tattoo that glowed during emotional

breakdowns.

5. Baguette the Beige – Was a baguette.

6. Flornt the Forgetful – Kept misplacing his own existence.

7. Ermintrude the Possibly Imaginary – Appeared only when no one looked directly at her.

They stared at Buttermunch. Buttermunch stared back.

Then he announced:
"I am here to join your sacred council, unlock your chaotic secrets, and possibly recruit you to fight a puffin army."

They whispered among themselves.

Rhyma finally spoke:
"You are not wizard, nor spellbound or sage,
But your beard radiates a mystical rage.
We accept you, goat of curious flair
But you must prove yourself... by summoning a chair."

The Summoning

"...A chair?" Grimbold asked, peeking from behind a bookcase.

"It's harder than it sounds," said Mistress Featherella. "Last week someone summoned a lizard with upholstery."

Buttermunch cleared his throat, spun dramatically in a circle, and stomped.

POP.
A chair appeared.
It had three legs, smelled of regret, and softly whispered "I'm tired" whenever someone sat on it.

"Acceptable," the Council declared.

Secrets, Scrolls, and One Unhelpful Prophecy

They showed Buttermunch the sacred scrolls of Slightly Off-Brand Magic™, including:
- The Great Binder of Bureaucratic Spells
- The Shampoo Codex
- How to Summon a Storm Using Only Sass and String Cheese

They also shared a troubling prophecy:
"When goat meets puffin at moonrise high,
One shall bleat, one shall cry,
And the squirrel will probably switch sides again."

"Sounds accurate," Buttermunch nodded.

Before leaving, Buttermunch swore an oath on the baguette (still unresponsive) and was gifted:
- A cape made of discontinued spell fabric
- A wand that doubles as a cheese grater

- And a title: "Honorary Misfit of the Arcane-ish Order."

As they ascended the stairs, Grimbold muttered, "So… what did we gain from this?"

Buttermunch replied, "Mystical allies. A cape. Possibly a carb-based familiar. And the knowledge that chairs are harder than they look."

Chad wept joyfully into a glitter scarf.

And somewhere in a puffin fortress…
King Puffin sensed magic rising.

Chapter Ten
The Realmsverse Spinoff Crossover Clause (Enforced by Chad)

It began innocently enough.

Chad had been reorganizing his glitter jars (by vibe, not colour) when he tripped over a scroll labelled: "Do Not Unseal: Realmsverse Crossover Clause 7.2b – Emotional Support Edition"

Naturally, he unsealed it immediately.
With a glitter pen.
While humming 'Let It Goat.'

The scroll screamed. Literally.

Then the sky changed colour, time blinked, and the group was suddenly... somewhere else.

Welcome to the Spinoff

They awoke on cushions made of metaphors.
Incense swirled. The sun had sparkles. There were feelings in the air. Too many.

"Where are we?" Fizzlefrond groaned.

Chad clapped his hands. "YAY! We've activated the Crossover Clause. Welcome to The Llamas of Emotional Liminality!"

No one moved.

A llama in a velvet shawl approached. She had wise eyes, unbothered energy, and a name tag that read: "Dr. Velveta, LCSW (Licensed Camelid of Sacred Wellness)"

"Greetings," she said, voice like molasses and moonlight.
"You've all been transported here for emergency inter-narrative therapy."

"NO," Buttermunch declared. "I don't need therapy. I need snacks and a refund."

"Denial," said Dr. Velveta gently. "Common in goats. Please sit. Share your inner bleats."

Group Therapy Begins

The cast sat in a semi-circle. Everyone had a tiny clipboard. Even the shrub, who had somehow followed them.

"Let's go around the circle," Dr. Velveta said. "Name one unresolved emotion you've been repressing."

Grimbold: "Existential dread. And butter envy."
Fizzlefrond: "Murdery boredom. And mild affection I refuse to name."
Buttermunch: "None. I am an emotionally evolved goat."
*Pause. *
"…Fine. Occasionally, I feel overlooked and slightly lactose-intolerant."
Chad: "I feel sparkly."
The Squirrel (in disguise): "VENGEANCE. Wait… uh, I mean… anxiety."

Crossover Chaos

The llama summoned characters from other Realmsverse novellas:
- Whiff the confused unicorn, who believed this was his dentist appointment
- Gerald the Possessed Armchair, whose advice was legally binding
- Clarence the Cat (possibly a minor god), who knocked over Fizzlefrond's therapy tea and disappeared through a wall

Each character was assigned a trauma-buddy.

Buttermunch got Whiff. They shared an emotional trust fall. It went poorly.
Grimbold got the chair. He cried. The chair approved.

Chad ran the snack table and proclaimed himself "Snaccidental Healer of Hearts."
The Squirrel tried to sabotage everything by stuffing the suggestion box with acorns, but it only made them more popular.

The Realmsverse Codex Reactivates

Suddenly, Dr. Velveta's eyes glowed.

"You have grown," she said. "The Clause has been fulfilled. Emotional arcs have been semi-processed. You may now return… but beware. You are now canonically connected to all spinoffs."

"Wait, what does that mean?" Grimbold shouted as the world dissolved.

Chad smiled. "It means… sequels."

Back in Buttermunchia, they landed in a heap.
Covered in tea leaves.
Emotionally unstable.
And holding tiny pamphlets that read:
"Healing Hurts, But Also So Does Goat Yoga." – Dr. Velveta

In a distant novella, a llama sighed in satisfaction.
And somewhere in the Realms Codex, the page shimmered:

CROSSOVER: SUCCESSFUL.

DAMAGE: EMOTIONAL.

SNACKS: PROVIDED.

Chapter Eleven
The Haunted Contract and the Clause That Bites

It started, as most dangerous magical misadventures do, with a scroll that should have been filed in "DO NOT TOUCH."

But it was not. It was instead filed under "Goat Treat Recipes" due to a tragic clerical error caused by Chad attempting to alphabetise things using feelings.

So, when Buttermunch opened it looking for "Cinnamon Sage Oat Biscuits," he accidentally unleashed a Haunted Legal Clause.

The Scroll That Screamed

The parchment unrolled itself. Wind blew indoors. Somewhere, thunder dramatically happened despite no clouds being present.

The scroll screamed:
"YOU HAVE VIOLATED ARTICLE 13 OF THE REALMSVERSE NARRATIVE CODE. YOU SHALL NOW FACE... CONTRACTUAL CONSEQUENCES."

Then it bit Grimbold. Like, actually bit him. Left a papercut shaped like a passive-aggressive ellipsis.

Enter: Buttermunch 2.0 (Now With Extra Ego)

Out of thin air, the contract shimmered and summoned a clone of Buttermunch.

But not just any clone. This version was:
- Twice as shiny
- Wearing a monocle
- Speaking in third person
- And calling himself "Sir Buttermagnus the Second, Esq."

"Behold!" he announced. "I am your better in hoof, wit, and beard oil application!"

Buttermunch narrowed his eyes. "You don't even moisturise properly."

The gauntlet was thrown. The goats prepared to hoof-wrestle for narrative dominance.

Meanwhile: Grimbold and the Gavel

Grimbold, dazed from being bitten by paper, had wandered off and found himself on trial in a courtroom made entirely of forgotten plot devices.

The judge? A sentient gavel named Judge Bonk.

"Order!" Bonk shouted. "You are accused of accessory to narrative fraud!"

"I don't even know what that is!" Grimbold cried.

"Then we'll begin with opening arguments," said the courtroom wall, which was somehow also a lawyer.

Grimbold had no legal team. Only a pamphlet from Chad that said: "Just sparkle confidently."

Hoof-Wrestle of Destiny

Buttermunch and Sir Buttermagnus squared off atop the Sacred Table of Slightly Wobbly Fate.

- Round One: Tie
- Round Two: Sir Buttermagnus recited poetry while flexing
- Round Three: Buttermunch headbutted a metaphor and won

At that moment, the cursed scroll tried to rewrite the ending by biting itself, which caused a narrative paradox.

Dr. Velveta (still canonically connected via crossover clause) appeared in a shimmer of therapeutic mist.

"You can't fight yourself," she said. "You must negotiate with the part of you that craves control."

"I crave snacks," Buttermunch said.

"Exactly," said Dr. Velveta.

The clone dissolved in a puff of glitter and tax returns.

Courtroom Climax

Just as Judge Bonk was about to sentence Grimbold to 47 hours of interpretive mime law, Buttermunch arrived with an override clause.

He hoof-stamped it. The courtroom exploded into confetti. Grimbold was cleared of all charges, and Bonk became a decorative doorstop in Chad's therapy hut.

They returned home slightly traumatised, but with:
- One less goat clone
- One less gavel nemesis
- And one more reason not to read magical goat treat recipes without supervision.

The scroll re-rolled itself and whispered:
"CLAUSE FULFILLED. CONSEQUENCES POSTPONED. SNACKS RECOMMENDED."

Chapter Twelve
The Inter-Realm Bake-Off Disaster

It was supposed to be diplomatic.

A gentle cultural exchange. A peace offering, even.

Instead, it became a pastry-based declaration of war.

The Setup

The Realms Council of Arbitrary Festivities (RC-AF) had announced the first-ever Inter-Realm Bake-Off, to be held in the Sacred Arena of Yeast.

Each realm would submit its finest culinary champion:
- The Elves sent Chef Lorithien, who spoke only in syllabic reduction and sourdough starters.
- The Dwarves sent Hilda the Hammerbaker, whose cookies could chip teeth and solve treaties.
- The Puffin sent... himself. With a suspicious pie.

And Buttermunch, naturally, volunteered without consulting anyone.
"I once ate a flaming scroll," he said. "I am clearly qualified."

Round One: The Pie Incident

The rules were simple: One pie. One hour. No poison.

Everyone ignored that last part.

The Puffin arrived with a Suspicious Crusty Delight
filled with something green and hissing.
"Family recipe," he winked. "Passed down by
enemies."

Buttermunch responded with a flaming cheese
soufflé that burned the judge's eyebrows clean off.
"Presentation: ten," said Judge Gerald (a possessed
armchair).

Then the Puffin's pie tried to bite someone.

Chaos ensued.

The Kitchen Spirit Appears

In the aftermath of the pie's attempted manslaughter,
someone (probably Chad) knocked over the Sacred
Salt Circle of Whisked Protection.
This summoned a Kitchen Spirit named Siftoria.

She appeared in a puff of rosemary and contractual
disapproval.

"WHO UNLEASHED THE UNSANCTIONED PIE
SPIRIT?" she boomed.
"It was the puffin," whispered Grimbold, hiding under
a pudding.

Siftoria turned to the group, holding a whisk like a gavel.

"I demand better working conditions, union rates, and a break every 45 soul minutes."

"You're a ghost," said Fizzlefrond.

"Exactly," said Siftoria. "Do you think this apron irons itself?"

Buttermunch's Counterattack

As Siftoria lectured the judges about ethereal labour rights, Buttermunch seized the moment.

"I present: The Goat's Blazing Gâteau!"

It was:
- Flaming
- Frosted
- Possibly sentient
- And delivered via interpretive dance

As the Gâteau twirled and exploded in sparkles, it punched the Puffin's pie square in the filling.

A hush fell over the arena.
Even Siftoria applauded.

The Verdict

Judge Gerald declared it a draw, which upset everyone.

Siftoria unionised the cutlery and vanished with half the kitchen.
The Puffin was banned from further baking.
And Buttermunch was awarded a golden oven mitt and a mysterious coupon that read:
"Redeem in case of future frosting emergencies. Valid in all ten realms. Not valid for necromantic eclairs."

They left sticky, victorious, and slightly traumatised.

The bake-off was never held again.

Chapter Thirteen
The Return of King Barktholomew the Leafy

The tree is back. It's leafy. It's petty. It wants custody of the crown and visitation rights to the meadow.

Court is held in a grove. All parties are legally required to wear moss.

King Barktholomew, once believed to have retired into serene root-based wisdom, had in fact been quietly stewing literally in a bog of spite and sap.

"I planted that crown myself," he declared as he emerged from the undergrowth, shedding acorns like threats.

Grimbold whispered, "Is it weird that I find him majestic?"

Buttermunch, however, was unimpressed. "Your bark is loud, but your contract's expired."

The Tree scoffed. It echoed like a forest holding a grudge.

Chad, acting as a freelance forest mediator, brought everyone tiny moss capes and a copy of the 'Realm Custody Guidelines for Sentient Flora.'

"According to subsection Root Nine," Chad intoned, "leafy monarchs may petition for crown proximity during equinox weekends, pending dramatic flair and at least one interpretive poem."

King Barktholomew immediately began a spoken-word oak lament.

Meanwhile, Buttermunch was fashioning a crown made of cheese rind and spite.

The trial escalated.

- The Puffin objected on the grounds of general inconvenience.
- The Squirrel tried to climb the Tree mid-ruling.
- Grimbold attempted to represent Buttermunch legally, using only charades.

The Grove Court recessed when a sudden gust of wind spread glitter across the judge stump, summoning Siftoria the Kitchen Spirit (again), who declared:
"IF I HAVE TO ARBITRATE ONE MORE MAGICAL CUSTODY HEARING, I SWEAR I'LL CURSE THE ENTIRE HERB GARDEN."

Everyone promptly reached a compromise:
- King Barktholomew gets shared symbolic custody of the crown.
- The meadow is declared a neutral peace zone.
- And Buttermunch has to wear a commemorative leaf brooch for one week.

The tree seemed satisfied.
It sank back into the earth with a rustling sigh, muttering something about sap royalties.

And just like that, another day in the Realms ended in mostly-mossy, moderately legal resolution.

Chapter Fourteen
The Great Goat Escape and the Realms' Most Wanted

Buttermunch is imprisoned in a magical holding orb for 'unauthorised realm manipulation.' He insists it was 'enthusiastic detouring.'

The orb is made of highly pressurised plot devices and smells vaguely of cinnamon.

Grimbold tries to argue with the guards but accidentally barters away his own shoes.

Chad appears briefly to offer spiritual coaching and a podcast link.
Neither helps.

It looks grim until Grimbold begins to cry.

Real tears. Of sadness. And slight dairy withdrawal.

This activates the orb's *Sympathy Trigger*, which was originally installed for emergency bard trauma but works in this case anyway.

Buttermunch, sensing an opportunity, delivers a heartfelt monologue:

"Cheese is more than curdled ambition it is unity, melted atop the casserole of community."

He then uses a **bent spoon**, stolen from Chad's smoothie pouch, to reflect light from the orb walls into a **mirror dimension loophole. **

The orb flickers.
A dramatic shimmer erupts.
Then... freedom.

Buttermunch lands squarely on the back of a runaway puffin and rides off into the chaos.

Wanted posters go up across the ten realms:
- WANTED: Enchanted Goat
- Crimes: Cheese Propaganda, Emotional Tampering, and Smuggling Unregistered Scrolls
- Last seen: Laughing maniacally while galloping through a council meeting

Chad updates the podcast.
Grimbold finds his shoes.
And somewhere in the distance, the sound of goat laughter echoes into legend.

The legend continues. Prepare your hooves, snacks, and possibly a legal waiver because **Buttermunch is BACK** *for Chapters 15–20 in the next Realmsverse goat-powered adventure:*

Volume II: "The Goatfather Returns"

Chapter Fifteen
The Goatfather Returns (And He Wants a Boat)

Buttermunch declares himself "The Goatfather of All Realms."

In a speech delivered while standing atop a soapbox made entirely of salted cheese wheels, he demands tribute:

- Three barrels of mead
- Four wheels of cheese
- And at least one ornamental canoe (for prestige)

Grimbold, who was just trying to eat his breakfast potato, is once again recruited into the madness.

Buttermunch gathers a crew:
- A gang of exiled pastry pirates (famous for stealing tarts and hearts)
- A talking whisk named Gregory who only speaks in baking metaphors
- And a cursed sea chart that occasionally screams

Their mission? A peaceful vacation cruise.
Their reality? A realm-wide manhunt launched within 3.5 hours of departure.

The vessel? A goat-powered yacht, modestly named
"The Legal Grey Area."

Decorated in dubious paperwork, enchanted sails,
and motivational posters stolen from Chad's therapy
hut, it glides through the inter-realm sea of mild
regret.

Buttermunch appoints himself:
- Captain
- Admiral of All Cheeses
- and Acting Director of Shipboard Snacks

The voyage begins with a toast of fermented cabbage
fizz and a dramatic reading of maritime goat law.

By nightfall, they've already been pursued by:
- The Realms Coast Guard (R.C.G.)
- Three mildly cursed swans
- And a mysterious shadow shaped suspiciously like
Odin

Buttermunch laughs in defiance. "LET THEM COME!"
he bleats.
Then slips on a decorative pineapple and falls
overboard.

Gregory the Whisk sighs.
Grimbold jumps in after him.

Day one ends, as most Buttermunch adventures do
dripping wet, wildly off-course, and somehow closer
to myth than ever before.

Chapter Sixteen
The Realm Voyage of the Mildly Cursed Map

The morning after the pineapple incident, Buttermunch and Grimbold dry off by the enchanted fireplace, which smells faintly of regret and cinnamon toast.

Gregory the Whisk presents the crew with a tattered, soup-stained scroll that screams when unfolded and weeps softly when no one pays attention to it.

"Behold," says Gregory. "The Map of Mildly Cursed Realms."

No one knows how it works. Chad once used it to find inner peace. Odin once used it as a napkin.

When held upside down and gently wept upon, the map reveals a blinking route to the legendary Isle of Misplaced Side Quests, a place where abandoned plot arcs roam free and dramatic lighting is always available.

Buttermunch is intrigued. "We sail at once," he declares, accidentally knocking over a cheese wheel with his enthusiasm.

The Legal Grey Area creaks heroically as it turns toward the coordinates blinking in dramatic italics.

As the crew sails on, they pass:
- A floating marketplace run by sentient octopus' scarves
- A sea rave hosted by water elementals with commitment issues
- And a storm made entirely of badly written exposition

Grimbold tries to steer. But the wheel is enchanted to only respond to emotional vulnerability. He is unsuccessful.

Instead, the yacht is navigated by Buttermunch's dramatic bleating and the map's occasional rhyming couplets.

At dusk, a signpost appears, floating in midair: "WELCOME TO THE ISLE OF MISPLACED SIDE QUESTS – Please Keep All Plot Devices Inside the Boat."

The map bursts into flames, sings a sea shanty, and explodes into glitter.

Buttermunch simply nods. "Perfect."

Chapter Seventeen
The Isle of Misplaced Side Quests
(And the Dramatic Penguin Prince)

The Legal Grey Area glides into the shimmering cove of the Isle of Misplaced Side Quests.

It is immediately obvious this island is... different.

Half-finished bridges lead nowhere. A group of retired background characters sun themselves beside a plot hole. Time loops once, hiccups, and then continues like nothing happened.

A dramatic breeze announces the arrival of Prince Reginald of the Ice Shelf, an emotionally unavailable penguin wearing a velvet cape and carrying a locket full of unresolved plotlines.

"You have entered the realm of forgotten arcs," he intones.
"Welcome. Also, beware of the sentient salad cult."

Buttermunch bows, mostly to show off his new ceremonial goat armour (made of pastry shells and irony).

Grimbold, meanwhile, gets cornered by a subplot involving an enchanted breadstick who wants revenge on the baguette that stole its destiny.

Gregory the Whisk is offered a chair on the island's Council of Impractical Magicians. He accepts, but only if snacks are included.

The salad cult appears. They chant things like "Lettuce ascend!" and "All hail the crouton king!"

Things spiral.

By nightfall, the crew has:
- Accidentally joined three musical numbers
- Disbanded the cult by offering them soup
- Declared Buttermunch a temporary Duke of Side Plots

Reginald nods approvingly. "That went better than expected."

A comet passes overhead. It whispers, "Next chapter," and no one questions it.

Chapter Eighteen
The Salad Rebellion and the Rise of Duke Buttermunch

Duke Buttermunch (a title he gave himself with great ceremony and zero oversight) decides it is time to govern.

He commissions a royal decree written entirely in hoofprints and glitter.
The first law: No salad shall be sentient without a license.

This does not go well.

The Salad Cult, still resentful despite the soup incident, stages a peaceful protest.
They hold signs like:
- "Let Romaine Rule"
- "End Lettuce Discrimination"
- "We Are Rooted, Not Ruled"

Prince Reginald attempts diplomacy by offering them croutons.
This only escalates things.

Meanwhile, Grimbold is put in charge of royal correspondence. He writes exactly one letter, which simply says, "Please stop" and includes a poorly drawn potato.

Gregory the Whisk insists on creating a new holiday: Whiskmas. It involves pudding, interpretive baking, and wearing hats made of dough.

As the rebellion gains momentum, Buttermunch prepares for a grand debate against the Salad Cult's charismatic leader: Sir Kalevin, Lord of Greens.

The debate is held in an open field. Attendance is mandatory. Seating is haybale.
Sir Kalevin arrives wearing a cape made of spinach and fury.

Buttermunch arrives riding a wheel of aged Gouda.

Arguments are exchanged. So are interpretive dances. A small musical breaks out.

In the end, a compromise is reached:
- Sentient salads must be registered
- Croutons may apply for citizenship
- And all future decrees must pass through the Committee of Reasonable Chaos

Everyone cheers. Mostly because snacks are provided.

Buttermunch retires to his cheese throne and contemplates what title to invent next.

Chapter Nineteen
The Committee of Reasonable Chaos
(And the Slightly Possessed Cabbage)

Buttermunch, now Duke, Cheese Regent, and
Honorary Ambassador of Breadsticks, is summoned
to appear before the Committee of Reasonable Chaos.

The Committee meets quarterly, biannually, and
whenever someone yells, "This is getting out of hoof!"

It consists of:
- A disgruntled prophecy pigeon
- Chad (who brought glitter for 'vibe balance')
- A haunted cabbage named Gerald
- And someone who may or may not be Thor wearing
a disguise and fake moustache

Buttermunch arrives late, citing 'existential ennui'
and a cheese-tasting emergency.

The cabbage begins to speak. In Latin. While spinning.
Everyone nods as if this is normal.

Gregory the Whisk presents a five-point plan for
chaos management, including:
1. Fewer exploding ducks
2. Stricter baguette licensing

3. More jazz flute
4. Less interpretive litigation
5. Mandatory snack breaks

Chad adds, "...and maybe goat bathhouses?"
No one agrees. But no one disagrees, either.

Grimbold attempts to read the minutes but
accidentally invokes a minor time loop.
The Committee agrees to table everything for a later
date, preferably after lunch.

As they adjourn, the cabbage gives Buttermunch a
warning:
"Beware the coming of the Lemon Law."
Then it faints.

No one knows what it means. But it sounds
important. And slightly citrusy.

Buttermunch begins plotting his next move... while
ordering a monocle and velvet cape online.

Chapter Twenty
The Lemon Law Cometh (And So Does the Unexpected Kangaroo Court)

The sky cracks open like an overripe melon. A single citrusy ray of doom shines through.

It is the coming of...
**The Lemon Law. **

No one knows what it does. But everyone is fairly certain it smells zesty and threatens bureaucratic calamity.

A royal decree arrives, carried by an extremely smug crow wearing reading glasses:
"By order of Article 9¾ of the Realmsverse Legal Appendix, Buttermunch is hereby summoned to... a kangaroo court."

It is not metaphorical.
The judge is an actual kangaroo in robes.
His name is Justice Bouncewell.
He has strong opinions on cheese-related anarchy.

The courtroom is held in a travelling tent that smells like lemons and judgment.
Grimbold attempts to defend Buttermunch using

interpretive dance.
Gregory the Whisk files a counter-lawsuit against gravity.
Chad offers Bouncewell a kombucha latte and gets held in contempt (again).

The charges:
- Unlicensed realm manipulation
- Possession of haunted produce
- Disrupting the fourth wall without a permit
- Goat-based constitutional rewrites

Buttermunch's defence?
He eats the lemon scroll.

A gasp.
A moment of citrus-scented silence.
Justice Bouncewell stares.
Then nods.
> "Court adjourned. This was nonsense anyway."

Celebration erupts.
Chad declares it "National Glitter Amnesty Day."
The cabbage blinks awake.
Whispers: "It has only begun..."
Then falls asleep again.

Buttermunch boards the Legal Grey Area.
And sails into the horizon.
To be continued...

BOOK
TWO

THE
GOATFATHER'S
GRAND TOUR

A Realmsverse Sequel to
The Enchanted Goat of Buttermunch

"Treason, Tapas, and Travel
Insurance (*Probably Not in That Order*)"

**Let's kick off Book Two: The Goatfather's
Grand Tour
with a Prologue that sets the scene in full
Realmsverse chaos...**

Here we go!

Prologue:

"In Which a Cruise Ship Is Commissioned Without a Single Qualified Crew Member"

Somewhere between the Sea of Reasonably Warm Tea
and the Archipelago of Mild Regrets,
a floating diplomatic incident is being assembled.

The vessel?

A goat-powered cruise yacht named
The Legal Grey Area
complete with bedazzled sails, a cheese vault, and a
spa that's mostly just warm glitter in buckets.

At the helm:
Buttermunch self-appointed Goatfather, naval
strategist, and "Certified Travel Shaman" (certificate
pending).

With him:
 • Grimbold, newly promoted to "Reluctant
First Mate"

• Gregory the Whisk, now moonlighting as Chief Nautical Counsel
• Chad, who brought sunscreen and 47 crystal-infused beach towels
• And a squirrel. Possibly Loki's. Possibly just a squirrel.

Their mission?

A "diplomatic grand tour" of the Ten Realms, to:

- Smooth over recent inter-realm lawsuits
- Return several borrowed (stolen) artifacts
- And most importantly:
  o Sample every type of realm-based tapas available to goat- kind.

The only problem?

The ship has no rudder.
No map.
And Chad thinks "navigation" is a type of herbal tea.

Still, the Realms need hope.
Or distraction.

And Buttermunch?
He's bringing both.
With snacks

Chapter One
"Of Tapas, Treason, and the Tax Evasion Mermaid"

The Legal Grey Area (now only partially on fire) glided into the waters of the Realm of Mild Fiscal Irregularities.

Buttermunch stood proudly at the helm, wearing a captain's hat made from a folded map and confidence.

"We sail for diplomacy!" he declared, "And also cheese-based hors d'oeuvres!"

On deck:
- Grimbold tried to read the official itinerary but found only a doodle of a goat eating the moon.
- Chad was giving emotional support yoga lessons to a suspiciously angry anchor.
- Gregory the Whisk was lawyering at a seagull.
- And the Squirrel was already building a tiny courtroom out of biscuits.

Then she arrived.

The Mermaid.

Wearing pearls, glittering scales, and holding a tax audit scroll.

"You are in violation of inter-realm income declarations," she sang, "And also, your goat owes twelve years of backpay on self-employment."

Buttermunch narrowed his eyes.

"I demand trial by tapas."

The mermaid blinked.

Then shrugged.

"Fine. But if I win, I claim the ship and one emotional support goblin."

Chad waved politely from a sea hammock.

The tapas were prepared.
Flaming brie.
Runic hummus.
A goat-shaped cake that may or may not have been alive.

The trial had begun.

IN LEGAL TROUBLE?
BETTER CALL BUTTERMUNCH!
1-800-GOAT-LAW

Chapter Two
"The Legal Grey Area vs. The Concept of Reality"

The ship had drifted off-course.

Possibly because its compass was replaced with a motivational rock that said, "Follow your dreams."

Buttermunch was mid-strategy session with the ship's figurehead (a talking loaf of bread named Susan), when reality itself began to flicker.

One moment: Sunny skies.
The next: Chad was floating in an existential jelly cube singing "Enya, but louder."

Gregory the Whisk emerged from below deck holding a glowing scroll.

"We've broken something," he whispered.
"Possibly time. Definitely causality. Maybe brunch."

Grimbold looked up from his attempt to chart the stars using leftover goat cheese.

"Can we un-break it?"

Gregory nodded solemnly.
"Only through a court case."

Thus began the trial between the ship and Reality itself.

Presiding Judge:
The Honourable Madame Absurdia, a sentient top hat with tenure.

Opening arguments were delivered by Buttermunch, using only bleats, interpretive hoof gestures, and something legally referred to as "moist logic."

Reality's defence was… Reality.
It mostly wept in binary and filed complaints about goat-scented dimensional rifts.

Chad offered to mediate.
Instead, he accidentally summoned an alternate version of the ship where everyone was a decorative spoon.

They were very polite.
And very pointy.

The case was settled when Buttermunch promised not to sue the fabric of space-time again,
and Reality agreed to "try harder not to unravel."

Result?

The ship was gifted a glowing truce amulet...
which Gregory immediately used as a disco ball.

Because priorities.

GOAT LAW
SCHOOL
LEARN IN
3 BLEATS OR LESS
CALL 1-800-GOAT-LAW

Chapter Three
"The Curse of Captain Crouton and the Baguette Mutiny"

It began, as these things often do, with a haunted breadbasket.

Buttermunch, ever the culinary visionary, had insisted on a mid-ocean feast themed "Croutons and Consequences."

Chad, wearing his self-assigned title "Sommelier of Starch," unveiled the centrepiece:
A crusty, slightly glowing baguette wearing a pirate hat.

"This," he said proudly, "is Captain Crouton."
"He's mostly carbs and entirely cursed."

The baguette blinked.
Then it sang.

A shanty so stale and crummy, every biscuit on board filed a complaint.

Gregory the Whisk began lawyering at the loaf, citing maritime grain codes.

But it was too late.
Captain Crouton had risen.

And he had followers:
- A gang of cinnamon scrolls with tiny swords.
- Two rebellious sourdoughs.
- And a gluten-free cracker with something to prove.

Grimbold tried diplomacy.
The baguette bit him.

The mutiny was swift.
By dusk, the cheese vault was under siege,
the spa was foaming with rage, and the mast had been
replaced by a breadstick.

Buttermunch bellowed from the helm:
"You want this ship, Crouton? You'll have to knead me
first!"

Then he launched himself into battle, wielding two
butter knives and an unreasonable amount of garlic.

The duel was epic.
Flour flew.
Dough wept.

Eventually, Buttermunch cast a binding spell using
ancient yeast chants and sealed Crouton in a jar
labelled:
"DO NOT OPEN. Especially if hungry."

The crew rejoiced.
The breadbasket was banished.

But far below deck...
the cracker was still whispering...
and plotting.

CAPTAIN CROUTON'S
PIRATE BREAD
SCHOOL
LEARN DOUGH LAW
SHANTIES & SABOTAGE
ARRR-IS

Chapter Four
"The Cheese Tribunal of Realm 7B (And the Missing Brie Defence)"

Realm 7B, known for its judicial fondue pits and legal cheese-based hierarchies, had summoned the crew of The Legal Grey Area for a tribunal.

Charges:
- Unauthorised dairy diplomacy
- Excessive fondue-related metaphors
- Theft of one (1) wheel of enchanted brie

The courtroom was a cavernous cellar, lit by glow-mould chandeliers and presided over by:
Judge Camemberta the Unmeltable, a no-nonsense gorgonzola with robes made of wax paper and a monocle of peppercorn.

Buttermunch acted as his own defence lawyer.

Naturally.

His strategy?
"Just smell how innocent I am."

Grimbold tried to help by presenting "Exhibit A: A Cheese That Definitely Isn't Cursed."

The cheese immediately hissed and turned into a small goat.
The gallery applauded.

Gregory the Whisk filed an emergency motion for "Trial by Snack," citing an obscure fondue clause.
The judge considered.
Then nodded gravely.

Snack-based justice commenced.

The court was presented with:
- Spicy cheddar arguments
- A rebuttal in the form of blue cheese crumbles
- And one extremely persuasive wheel of Gouda in a wig

In closing arguments, Buttermunch licked the prosecution's evidence table.
"Your Honour," he said, "this brie is store bought. Checkmate."

Verdict?
Not guilty.
But only because the real thief was revealed to be:
Captain Crouton's ghost, who'd hidden the brie under Chad's meditation mat.

The court ruled:
- Brie returned.

- Ghost mildly banished.
- Goat allowed to keep wearing the powdered wig.

Chapter Five
"The Accidental Marriage Pact of Glitter Island (And the Squirrel's Best Man Speech)"

It started with a glitter explosion and ended with a legally binding ceremony no one remembers agreeing to.

Such is the way of Glitter Island, the only known location where:
- Confetti is a legal tender,
- Vows can be shouted over karaoke,
- And accidentally saying "I do" while sipping a glitter smoothie counts in triplicate.

Buttermunch had arrived to negotiate a trade deal involving glow-in-the-dark cheese rinds.
Chad came for the vibes.
Grimbold came because he wasn't allowed to stay on the boat unsupervised anymore.

Unfortunately, the locals mistook their arrival as part of the Annual Matrimonial Melee Festival, a Realms tradition where contestants are randomly assigned soulmates for sport, spectacle, and tax purposes.

One hiccup later (and a spilled glitter scroll), and Buttermunch was declared spiritually wed to... the Squirrel.
Legally. Emotionally. Ceremonially.

The Squirrel gave a best man speech at its own wedding.
It included:
- A roast of every crew member
- A slideshow of Buttermunch's most embarrassing moments (with music)
- And a dance number featuring 12 flamingos and Chad in a veil

Gregory the Whisk tried to object but was silenced by the ceremonial gavel, which also doubled as a tinsel cannon.

By sunset, the island was covered in sparkles, the goat was technically royalty, and Grimbold had accidentally married a decorative shrub.

"This," Buttermunch declared, "is why I hate ceremonies."

Then he did the conga with a coconut priest and filed for annulment via interpretive hula.

Chapter Six
"The Contract of Confetti and the Bureau of Binding Festivities"

The morning after the matrimonial melee, Buttermunch woke up beneath a gazebo made entirely of candy floss and bad decisions.

Next to him:
- A glitter cannon
- A legally binding scroll in the shape of a balloon animal
- And Chad, who was furiously meditating in a tub of rainbow jelly

The Squirrel (now wearing a sash that read "Officially Entangled") was already lobbying for joint goat-squirrel holidays and a reality show deal.

But the worst part?
A knock at the invisible door.
The Bureau of Binding Festivities had arrived.

They were bureaucrats.
With clipboards.
And matching sparkly robes.

Their mission:
To ensure that all festive incidents, especially goat-based ones, were registered, certified, and enforced across all realms.

Failure to comply would result in:
- Ban from future Realmsverse celebrations
- Revocation of party privileges
- And mandatory attendance at a Goblin-hosted grievance seminar ("So You've Married a Rodent")

Buttermunch, of course, tried to argue.
"I never knowingly signed anything!"
"You drooled on the scroll," the lead inspector replied.
"That counts as intent."

Grimbold attempted to stall them by offering snacks and asking complicated tax questions.
Gregory the Whisk cited the "Whisk Exemption Clause," which didn't exist, but sounded fancy.

Meanwhile, Chad activated a failsafe:
Confetti Distraction Protocol #47.

Suddenly, sparkles filled the air, the Bureau lost all their pens, and someone (probably Chad) released a live unicorn wearing a judge's wig.

In the chaos, Buttermunch:
- Ate the original scroll,

- Declared diplomatic immunity,
- And rode the unicorn straight into the Fountain of Questionable Clarity.

Whether the Bureau would return was uncertain.

But one thing was clear:
That scroll was definitely not gluten-free.
And the Squirrel had already printed wedding invitations.

Chapter Seven
"The Realm of Forgotten Holidays (And the Inconvenient Resurrection of Pancake Day)"

It began, as many catastrophes do, with Chad sneezing on a map.

Unfortunately, it was a magical map. And even more unfortunately... the sneeze activated a realm jump.

One glittery blink later, the entire crew of The Legal Grey Area found themselves in:

Realm 7¾ – The Realm of Forgotten Holidays.

Where every festival too weird, too niche, or too inconvenient goes to retire.

They were immediately greeted by:
- A sentient Groundhog with commitment issues
- A council of bitter Cupids in sweatpants
- And a mime protest against "National Noise Appreciation Week"

But the most dangerous thing?

Pancake Day.

Long banished for "unholy levels of syrup stickiness" and a war crime involving jam, Pancake Day had been quietly waiting for its return.

And Buttermunch just gave it a reason.

How?

He flipped a ceremonial flapjack using only his hooves... and landed it. Perfectly. In front of the Grand Spatula of Celebration.

This act:
- Revived the holiday
- Reignited ancient food rivalries
- And triggered The Great Syrup Summoning

By dusk, the skies were raining lemon zest, and the Squirrel was leading a pancake rebellion against "Crepe Supremacy."

Grimbold got stuck to a flagpole. Gregory the Whisk declared martial law over all condiments. And Chad... was worshipped as the "Prophet of Butter."

The Realm itself began to crack.

Holidays reawakened across the calendar:
- "Apologise to Your Furniture Day"
- "National Lint Whispering"
- "Talk Like a Dragon Who's Had Dental Work Week"

Buttermunch did the only logical thing:

He offered the Grand Spatula a bribe of sentient maple syrup (named Kevin) and negotiated a ceasefire over waffles.

In the end, Pancake Day was placed back in containment. Kevin the Syrup became a Realmsverse diplomat.

And Buttermunch?

He swore off breakfast food... for at least two days.

Chapter Eight
"The Lint Uprising and the Return of the Sock Monarchy"

It started with static cling.

One moment, Chad was peacefully folding towels using his "Zen Origami Laundry" technique…
The next? A small pile of lint hissed at him and vanished under the couch.

"Is your fluff hissing again?" Grimbold asked, eating cereal out of a goblet.

Buttermunch didn't answer. He was too busy inspecting the ship's laundry chute, which now pulsed with suspicious energy and the faint scent of warm foot.

Suddenly: Boom. The laundry room exploded in a blizzard of rebellious fuzz.

Realm 6C, the Kingdom of Cozy Things, had declared war.

Specifically:
- The Sock Monarchy had returned from exile.
- Their goal: Reclaim the lost throne of Warmth and

Foot Security.
- Their first decree: All unmatched socks be reunited
by magical decree.

The lint? That was no ordinary laundry dust.

It was sentient fuzz, awakened by years of neglect and
the betrayal of single dryers.

Led by General Pompom, a battle-scarred bobble
from a 1980s beanie, they launched the Uprising of
the Unlaundered.

Grimbold was drafted into a fuzzball militia.
Gregory the Whisk was knighted "Sir Swirl-a-Lot" by
the Sock Queen herself.
And Buttermunch? He was placed on trial for Crimes
Against Cosiness, namely:
- Hoof holes in three sacred socks
- Unauthorised dryer vent spelunking
- And failing to bow during "The Ceremony of the
Sock Fold"

The court was brutal. The jury was mostly crocheted.

But right as sentencing began, Chad intervened.

Wearing a bathrobe of peace and wielding the Sacred
Fabric Softener Wand, he challenged the monarchy to:
"The Softening."

This ancient trial involved:
- A footrace across shag carpet,
- A diplomacy round in fuzzy slippers,
- And a final comfort duel via heated blanket.

Victory?

Buttermunch and Chad won... barely.
Mostly because the Sock King slipped on a rogue banana peel from last week's tapas buffet.

Peace was restored.

The Sock Monarchy agreed to share power with the Council of Comfy.
And the lint? It unionised.

Chapter Nine
"Of Ghost Spoons, Haunted Teacups, and the Dinner Party That Summoned Itself"

It began with a faint clinking.

Not the charming kind that suggests polite tea-drinking...
But the eerie, echoing clink of cutlery with unresolved trauma.

The Legal Grey Area had dropped anchor near Realm 4S½, a realm known only in whispers and poorly translated cookbook margins.

The realm's reputation?
- Ghost tableware.
- Cursed banquet halls.
- A dinner party that summons itself once a century and serves only the most awkward topics of conversation.

Naturally, Buttermunch RSVP'd 'yes' before anyone could stop him.

That night, the crew arrived at a haunted table floating in mist.

Each place setting was perfectly set.
Each fork... weeping.
Each chair... already whispering your deepest secrets.

Chad sat beside a haunted soup bowl named Lucinda.
Grimbold kept accidentally making eye contact with a
ghost ladle.
And Buttermunch?
He was loving it.
He declared himself 'Head Chef of the Spirit Feast'
and demanded ghost cheese.

Dinner was served, by no one.
It just... appeared.
So did the guests:
- A poltergeist who only speaks in riddles about
cutlery etiquette.
- The Ghost of Leftovers Past.
- And a possessed cheese wheel named Carl.

Halfway through the meal, the room voted to hold a
séance.
Gregory the Whisk hosted.

Spirits were summoned.
Secrets were spilled.
The teacups judged everyone.

Turns out, the dinner party wasn't haunted by
ghosts...
It was haunted by unresolved conversations.

So, Chad led a group therapy session over dessert.
Buttermunch forgave the butter knife who ghosted
him.
Grimbold made peace with his inner soup.

And Carl, the cheese wheel?
He got a job as a motivational speaker in Realm 8B.

The dinner ended in applause and passive-aggressive
applause from the cutlery drawer.
And thus, the curse was broken...
Until next century.

Chapter Ten
"The Time Loop Jacuzzi and the Goat Who Refused to Learn a Lesson"

In the glittery depths of Realm 3¾, where time occasionally hiccups and hot tubs sparkle with eldritch steam, there exists a place of legend:
The Time Loop Jacuzzi.

It promises rejuvenation, reflection, and just the right amount of interdimensional shrinkage.
What it delivers, however, is twenty-four straight hours of repeating the worst moment of your week...
But with loofahs.

Naturally, Buttermunch dove in hooves-first.
He wanted answers. Clarity. And possibly to soak his aching frog muscles.
Instead, he relived his argument with a sentient parking ticket on Loop 7.
Then again on Loop 8.
Then Loop 9, but this time with musical accompaniment.

Grimbold, suspicious of anything with bubbles and magical disclaimers, stayed poolside with goggles and a meat pie.

Chad, meanwhile, claimed he'd already ascended beyond time and was just here for 'quantum exfoliation.'

Gregory the Whisk was briefly trapped in a time-snarl involving unfinished baking instructions and an aggressive brownie recipe from 1984.

Each loop brought Buttermunch closer to the edge of enlightenment, of understanding, and of trying to headbutt the time vortex into behaving.

But what finally broke the loop?
Not wisdom.
Not inner growth.
But a goat scream so mighty it rewrote the Jacuzzi's magical source code.

Time sneezed.
Reality twitched.
And suddenly, it was Tuesday.

Everyone got out.
Everyone was pruney.
And no one wanted to talk about the karaoke incident from Loop 12.

Lesson learned?
Absolutely not.

Buttermunch declared the Time Loop Jacuzzi 'therapeutic-ish' and suggested franchising it.

Chad agreed.
Grimbold wept quietly into his pie.

And the Realms... sighed.
Because this goat? He was just getting started.

Chapter Eleven
"The Accidental Goat Cult and the Holy Order of Snackrifice"

It started, as most unexpected religions do, with a cheese wheel and a poorly worded thank-you note.

After escaping the Time Loop Jacuzzi, Buttermunch and his crew docked in a quiet coastal realm where goats were considered sacred…
Or possibly just fashionable. The details were fuzzy. Like the goats.

Buttermunch, in all his sparkly, goatish glory, was greeted by a group of robe-wearing locals who immediately declared him a divine being.
Why?
Because his arrival coincided with a spontaneous cheese storm.
And someone misread 'spa retreat' as 'prophesied hoofed redeemer.'

Chad leaned in immediately, accepting the role of 'Head Mystic of the Snackrifice Chamber.'
Grimbold protested, but accidentally gave a sermon on friendship and was promoted to 'Blessed Prophet of the Side Quests.'

Gregory the Whisk became a holy relic. He objected but was lovingly bedazzled anyway.

The cult, officially titled the *Holy Order of Snackrifice*, began performing rituals involving:
• sacred grazing,
• interpretive snacking,
• and chanting about the Miracle of the Goat Who Moonwalked on a Griddle.

Buttermunch was thrilled.
Finally, a realm that understood reverent snack timing.
Until...
A rival cult arrived: The Church of the Holy Chicken Nugget.
Their leader? Sir Clucks the Foul.

Negotiations escalated into a dance-off.
The goat cult chanted.
The chicken cult clucked.
Someone released confetti. Possibly Chad.

In the end, a treaty was signed, witnessed by a confused marshmallow and notarised by a waffle.
Both cults agreed to share Wednesdays and trade snack recipes every full moon.

Buttermunch left, crowned in corn chips and scented candles, a little confused but deeply moisturised.

And the Holy Order of Snackrifice?
They still bleat prayers at dusk.
Just in case.

Chapter Twelve
"The Emotional Support Kraken and the Realm of Seasonal Therapy"

As diplomatic tensions between snack-based cults cooled, Buttermunch found himself mysteriously summoned to the Realm of Seasonal Therapy.

It was a realm bathed in aromatherapy fog, lined with sentient pumpkins, and ruled by an oversized kraken named Clementine.
Not terrifying. Just large. And very, very emotionally available.

Clementine introduced herself as an official 'Emotional Support Kraken,' certified in:
• Weighted Tentacle Therapy
• Seaweed Journaling
• And Deep-Sea Breathing Exercises

She greeted Buttermunch with a squishy hug and a gentle, echoing voice that said, "You're seen. You're salted. You're safe."

Chad burst into tears immediately. Grimbold attempted to hide in a teacup. Gregory the Whisk began reprocessing past trauma from his mixing days.

Buttermunch, however, was having none of it.
"I have no unresolved emotional issues," he bleated, stomping confidently into the Therapy Labyrinth.

He emerged three hours later with glitter tears, a signed release form, and a new appreciation for scented kelp wraps.

The Realm of Seasonal Therapy worked fast.
There were warm cider fountains. Blanket burrito classes. And one extremely confrontational dandelion who insisted everyone talk about their feelings.

By the end of the day, Clementine the Kraken had assigned everyone a seasonal affirmation:
• Chad: "You are more than your mood board."
• Grimbold: "You deserve soft socks and hard boundaries."
• Gregory: "Your purpose is not just to stir, but to stand."
• Buttermunch: "You are not defined by the treaties you bleat."

Buttermunch didn't cry.
But he did sigh dramatically while watching the sunset from atop a kelp swing.

The crew left calmer, softer, and with several new seasonal tote bags.
Clementine waved all twelve of her arms goodbye.

And the Realms?

Briefly... they felt just a little more emotionally balanced.

Chapter Thirteen
"The Goatfather's Guide to Avoiding Accountability (With Bonus Map of Regrettable Detours)"

After the Realm of Seasonal Therapy, Buttermunch decided it was time to take control of the narrative. Mostly by avoiding it altogether.

He published a self-authored manifesto titled:
"The Goatfather's Guide to Avoiding Accountability."
Chapter highlights included:
• Blame the map.
• If you bleated it, deny it.
• Emotional honesty is best handled by other people.
• Detour until forgotten.

To accompany the guide, he distributed magical scrolls containing the **Bonus Map of Regrettable Detours**
a shimmering, ever-shifting parchment that actively led travellers away from responsibility.

Chad framed his.
Grimbold used his as a place mat.
Gregory the Whisk attempted to declare it a new continent.

Meanwhile, Buttermunch used the guide to escape no less than:
• Three inter-realm audits,
• Two ex-wives,
• And one very determined bard with a subpoena.

But as he stood on the deck of The Legal Grey Area, sipping a sparkling root beer and watching the sunset through magical opera glasses,
a question stirred in his soul:

**"What if I accidentally started a religion again?" **

He chose not to answer.
Instead, he drew a new route on the map labelled "Here Be Optional Consequences" and ordered the yacht to sail onward.

Chapter Fourteen
"The Return of the Forgotten Realm (Now With Extra Bureaucracy)"

Somewhere between a misfiled dimension and a
discontinued breakfast cereal aisle,
the Forgotten Realm blinked back into existence.

It returned with forms.
So many forms.

Declarations of Intent to Remember.
Applications for Provisional Memory Restoration.
Permit 42-B for Inter-Realm Acknowledgement.

Buttermunch was immediately detained by a
clipboard-wielding bureaucrat named **Trenchcoat
Fernwhistle**,
who insisted the goat's yacht had breached the
border between memory and mild inconvenience.

Grimbold tried reasoning.
Chad tried crystals.
Gregory the Whisk claimed diplomatic immunity on
behalf of the United Bakes of Yeastonia.

No one listened.

To escape, Buttermunch invoked Clause 9 of the
Realmsverse Travel Codex:
"If detained without snacks, one may summon a
Temporary Realm Diversion via interpretive
paperwork."

What followed was a glitter-drenched filing dance,
a squirrel-led distraction in the archives,
and the accidental creation of a Department of
Spontaneous Reclassification.

In the end, they were released on a technicality:
The Forgotten Realm had forgotten it had jurisdiction.

As they sailed away, Trenchcoat Fernwhistle yelled,
"You'll hear from our Realm Compliance Team!"

But Buttermunch just bleated, waved his hoof
dismissively,
and muttered, "Tell them to take a number."

Chapter Fifteen
"The Emotional Toll Booth of Realm Toll-9 (Now Accepting Existential Dread as Payment)"

As The Legal Grey Area glided into Realm Toll-9, the crew was met with an ornate booth floating in the sky.
It glowed faintly with bureaucratic menace and smelled vaguely of liquorice and regret.

Inside sat a toad in a waistcoat.
His name tag read: "Emotional Auditor: Gerald."

"Welcome to Toll-9," Gerald croaked,
"Please pay your fee in one of the following: gold, secrets, or unresolved trauma."

Grimbold offered a potato.
Chad tried to trade a crystal labelled "Regret of My Third Life Coach."
Gregory the Whisk attempted to sing a legal jingle.

But it was **Buttermunch** who finally stepped forward.

He bleated once, summoned a scroll, and declared:
"I hereby pay in full with my most existential bleat."

He then launched into an emotional soliloquy about
the fleeting nature of cheese,
the heartbreak of half-eaten pastries,
and the time he fell in love with a fondue fountain
that betrayed him.

Gerald blinked slowly, wiped away a single tear, and
stamped the passport.

"That'll do, goat. That'll do."

They passed through.
But none of them spoke for hours.
Except Chad, who asked if anyone wanted a group
hug and was immediately thrown overboard (again).

Chapter Sixteen
"The Snack Tribunal of Crumblefjord (And the Case of the Missing Macaron)"

The ship docked at Crumblefjord, where the cobblestone streets were paved with shortbread, and citizens wore biscuit hats to denote rank.

At the centre of town stood the Tribunal, an edible courthouse made entirely of gingerbread and stern glares.

Inside, chaos reigned.
Someone had stolen the Realm's prized macaron: a lavender-infused, 14-layer miracle allegedly blessed by pastry gods.

Buttermunch, now a self-declared 'Forensic Dessertologist,' took the lead.
He sniffed crumbs, interrogated éclairs, and grilled a scone under metaphorical heat.

Chad insisted it was a gluten-based spiritual crisis.
Gregory the Whisk objected to everything with great flair.

Suspicion fell on a suspiciously flaky tart named
Madame Crusté.
She claimed innocence, blaming a rogue wind and
existential hunger.

In the end, it was revealed that the macaron had not
been stolen...
...but offered itself as a diplomatic gift to the Realm of
Hungry Spirits.

All charges were dropped.
A new macaron was commissioned.
And Buttermunch was declared an honorary
Crumbmarshal of Crumblefjord.

He demanded a badge.
He got a biscuit.

Chapter Seventeen
"The Bureau of Magical Mislabels (And the Exploding Goat Perfume Debacle)"

The Legal Grey Area drifted into Realm Labela, home of the Bureau of Magical Mislabels.

The realm operated entirely on enchanted tags, stickers, and poorly translated warning labels. Unfortunately, Buttermunch had accidentally acquired a crate of what he believed to be "Goat Musk of Eternal Confidence."

It was actually "Combustible Essence of Spicy Ferret." Boom.

The resulting explosion not only singed the ship's sails,
but summoned a very confused perfume elemental who demanded royalties.

Chad tried to soothe it with essential oils and interpretive humming.
Gregory the Whisk wrote a cease and desist in whipped cream.

The Bureau investigated, but got distracted by a batch
of mislabelled jam that was actually a tiny volcano.

By the end of the week, Buttermunch had negotiated
a deal:
He would rename the perfume 'Goatfume:
Dangerously Bold'
and donate 3% of proceeds to the Society for
Labelling Accuracy.

The perfume elemental agreed.
And promptly vaporised the complaint department.

All things considered, it was a win.

Chapter Eighteen
"The Unexpected Pants Treaty of Realm Snug"

Upon arriving in Realm Snug, the crew was immediately issued mandatory pants.

Not armour. Not robes. Pants.

The realm had strict treaty-based dress codes, enforced by the League of Leggings and the Pantaloons Patrol.

Buttermunch was unimpressed.
He preferred his hooves free. Untethered. Dramatic.

Gregory the Whisk adapted quickly by fashioning a sash. Chad wore three pairs incorrectly.
Grimbold simply sighed and put on the allotted corduroy.

But the realm was in turmoil, a trade dispute with Realm Formalwear had triggered the Great Sock Rebellion.
Realm Snug needed a treaty, and Buttermunch, now dressed in golden fleece leggings (begrudgingly), was ready to negotiate.

After a dramatic summit involving sequined charts,
interpretive dance proposals, and a pants fashion
runway,
an accord was reached:
Realm Snug would keep its pants,
Realm Formalwear would accept sock-based taxation,
and Buttermunch would be declared honorary
Ambassador of Fabric Diplomacy.

He refused the title.
But kept the leggings.
They had pockets.

Chapter Nineteen
"The Goat, the Crown, and the Great Laundry Uprising"

It began with a missing sock.

One sock, to be precise. Royal. Embroidered. Mysteriously devoured by the palace washing manticore.

Buttermunch claimed diplomatic immunity. Chad blamed planetary alignment. Gregory the Whisk blamed Chad.

The realm revolted.
Laundry baskets overturned. Dryer spirits summoned. The Crown itself threatened to abdicate unless someone found the missing laundry token.

Grimbold, trying to mediate, got trapped in a sentient dryer set to 'eternal fluff'.

Buttermunch rallied the crew. He donned a cape made from mismatched socks and declared war on lint.

It was not a long war.
But it was loud.

After a dramatic trial involving fabric softener
testimonies and witness accounts from several rogue
towels,
Buttermunch was cleared of all charges and offered a
permanent crown position as High Spin Cycle
Overseer.

He declined.
But kept the cape.
And the sock.

It made a great puppet.

Chapter Twenty
"The Final Voyage of The Legal Grey Area (And the Realm That Wasn't There Yesterday)"

It was supposed to be a short voyage.

A farewell cruise. A last goat-powered hurrah.
Just one more tour around the moderately enchanted coastlines of Realm Seven-and-a-Half.

But then the fog rolled in.
The stars blinked sideways.
And the map developed a sarcastic new continent labelled: 'Here Be Consequences.'

The Legal Grey Area vanished for precisely 42 minutes and reappeared somewhere between time, tea, and tax season.
A new realm shimmered into existence, built entirely of misplaced paperwork, broken promises, and expired cheese.

Buttermunch declared it his final destination.
Grimbold wept quietly into a soggy atlas.
Chad meditated upside-down and renamed the island 'Closure Cove.'

The ship docked.
Treaties were waved in the air.
Goat hooves echoed on bureaucracy-marble as
Buttermunch approached a golden podium.

He cleared his throat.
Raised the sacred cheese scroll.
And said, with great and terrible majesty:

"We have arrived…
at a plot twist."

Epilogue
"The Realm, the Goat, and the Leftover Cheese"

It is said, mostly by Chad, that endings are just snack breaks between plotlines.

In the quiet aftermath of treaty-signings, dance-battles, and mysterious inter-realm cheese exchanges, The Legal Grey Area now floats peacefully between known story arcs.

Buttermunch has opened a School for Advanced Goat Rhetoric and Cheese Law.
Grimbold teaches Tapas Diplomacy on Tuesdays.
Chad runs weekly 'Let Go with Goat Yoga' sessions, featuring crystal-infused hummus.

The Squirrel? Still chaotic. Still probably on the roof.
And the forgotten realm?
Well... it's starting to remember itself. But only on weekends.

Somewhere, a map redraws itself in glitter.
A scroll re-rolls.
And Buttermunch, in full ceremonial beard butter, winks at the fourth wall and says:

"Next time… we bring snacks."

Deleted Scroll Excerpts from Buttermunch's Legal Files

EXHIBIT A: The Treaty of Slightly Regrettable Promises

"I, Buttermunch, being of mostly sound hoof and glitter-infused judgment, hereby promise not to claim dominion over Realm 7B unless:
(a) The current ruler forgets it exists,
(b) It's Tuesday,
or (c) I'm really in the mood for brie."

Signed in mead. Sealed with a hoofprint. Witnessed by a sleepy goblin named Clive.

EXHIBIT B: Goat Law Clause 17(c) "The Right to Dramatic Entry"

"All goats, enchanted or otherwise, may enter a courtroom, council, or coronation by:
• Bursting through double doors
• Riding a glitter cannon
• Or somersaulting through a stained-glass window shouting, 'OBJECTION!'"

Note: This clause does not apply to weddings. Except when it absolutely does.

EXHIBIT C: The Baguette Incident Settlement

"We, the Undersigned (and Slightly Singed), agree to forget the Great Baguette Mutiny of Realm 5's Bakery Court.
In exchange, Buttermunch will stop referring to himself as 'The Crustice of Peace.'"

This document may be void if anyone brings croissants into the courtroom again.

EXHIBIT D: The Snackrifice Immunity Motion

"No goat shall be held legally accountable for sacrifices made during midnight snack rituals, particularly those involving:
• A wheel of cheese
• Five dancing squirrels
• And an overly enthusiastic life coach named Chad."

This motion was accidentally passed twice due to duplicate scrolls printed on edible parchment.

Deleted Scroll Excerpts from Buttermunch's Legal Files

EXHIBIT A: The Treaty of Slightly Regrettable Promises

"I, Buttermunch, being of mostly sound hoof and glitter-infused judgment, hereby promise not to claim dominion over Realm 7B unless:
(a) The current ruler forgets it exists,
(b) It's Tuesday,
or (c) I'm really in the mood for brie."

Signed in mead. Sealed with a hoofprint. Witnessed by a sleepy goblin named Clive.

EXHIBIT B: Goat Law Clause 17(c) "The Right to Dramatic Entry"

"All goats, enchanted or otherwise, may enter a courtroom, council, or coronation by:
• Bursting through double doors
• Riding a glitter cannon
• Or somersaulting through a stained-glass window shouting, 'OBJECTION!'"

Note: This clause does not apply to weddings. Except when it absolutely does.

EXHIBIT C: The Baguette Incident Settlement

"We, the Undersigned (and Slightly Singed), agree to forget the Great Baguette Mutiny of Realm 5's Bakery Court.
In exchange, Buttermunch will stop referring to himself as 'The Crustice of Peace.'"

This document may be void if anyone brings croissants into the courtroom again.

EXHIBIT D: The Snackrifice Immunity Motion

"No goat shall be held legally accountable for sacrifices made during midnight snack rituals, particularly those involving:
• A wheel of cheese
• Five dancing squirrels
• And an overly enthusiastic life coach named Chad."

This motion was accidentally passed twice due to duplicate scrolls printed on edible parchment.

Supplementary Witness Statements

Clive the Goblin, Semi-Retired Notary

"I was definitely awake for most of it. The goat made some strong arguments. Also, there were snacks."

Sir Crumbs, Retired Pastry Knight

"The baguette was enchanted. I have no regrets. Except maybe the icing duel."

Princess Fizzlefrond

"I only signed because the goat promised me a realm-wide spa day. He delivered. Sort of. It involved glitter buckets."

LEAKED LEGAL NOTES

(Compiled by the Bureau of Magical Mislabels)

1. Clause 4.1 of the Treaty
of Slightly Regrettable Promises

1 was econd signature—purputtfud to writenn ın
acorn ink by a squirrel using its tail. Endılodeɾoɾd.

2. Snackrifice Immunity Motion

While legally passed, this scroll contains no verified
witnesses. Chad claims the scroll "signed itself" afte
an inspirational speech about manifesting boundatie

3. Baguette Incident Settlement

Signature #3 is just a dooólle of a cheese wheel
wearing sunglasses. The artist (yrebumewly sqʞired,
has nófoved by a nut trail.

4. Goat Law Clause 17(c)

Witness signature "Judge Snortlesnoot" appears to
be a psuedonym. Further investigation reveals it
was the squirrel again, in a monocle.

Cast of Characters – The Enchanted Goat of Buttermunch & The Goatfather's Grand Tour

Main Characters

Buttermunch

Enchanted goat. Trickster. Lawyer. Realtor. Naval commander.

Known for: Swagger, magical hoof tactics, and dramatic declarations.

Grimbold (or sometimes Eggthor)

Humble farm boy turned reluctant adventurer.

Known for: Potato farming, emotional breakdowns, and eternal loyalty.

The Divine & Dramatic

Odin

Bumbling, beardy, dramatic god-king.

Known for: Getting tricked. Repeatedly.

Princess Fizzlefrond

Sharp, sarcastic, sword-wielding royal.

Known for: Eye-rolls, intelligence, and questionable taste in goats.

King Barktholomew the Leafy

A sentient tree with legal opinions and vengeance issues.

Known for: Holding court in moss robes and fighting for crown custody.

Realmsverse Cameos & Magical Chaos Agents

Chad the Goblin Life Coach

Life coach, self-declared wizard of "manifestation," beach towel enthusiast.

Known for: Terrible advice, crystal-based plans, and emotional goat yoga.

Loki's Squirrel (a.k.a. The Squirrel)

Mischievous chaos agent. Occasionally a narrator. Always suspicious.

Known for: Forging documents, switching sides, and interpretive dance sabotage.

Gregory the Talking Whisk

Reformed enchanted kitchen tool turned nautical legal advisor.

Known for: Dramatic flourishes and heated courtroom whiskings.

Creatures, Villains & One-Off Legends

Sir Clucks the Foul

Terrifying feathered villain (guest villain in Book 1).

Known for: A cackle that echoes through realms.

The Puffin

Enchanted puffin. Possibly immortal. Very upset.

Known for: Revenge, lawsuits, and a surprisingly effective beak.

Captain Crouton

Cursed bread pirate. Haunts sea routes and gluten-free menus.

Known for: Leading the Baguette Mutiny and shouting "Crumbho!"

Support Characters & Absurd Bureaucrats

The Secret Council of Slightly Off-Brand Wizards

Includes:

- A wizard who speaks only in rhyme

- A magical baguette

- Probably Chad in disguise

The Emotional Support Kraken

Squishy, therapeutic, and unexpectedly wise.

Known for: Hug-based interventions.

The Bureau of Magical Mislabels

Bureaucratic nightmare with misfiled curses, mislabelled scrolls, and enchanted office supplies.

The Bureau of Binding Festivities

Responsible for magical weddings, confetti-related accidents, and festive chaos.

Bonus & Background Characters

- The Haunted Teacup

- Sock Royalty of Realm Snug

- Snack Tribunal Judges of Crumblefjord

- Existential Toll Booth Attendants

- Therapy Llama of the Crossover Clause

- Kraken Support Group (Realm of Seasonal Therapy)

- Sentient Gavel

- The Cheese Vault Keeper

- Forgotten Holiday Spirits (including Pancake Day)

- Laundry Uprising Leader (Lord Socksworth)

MAIN
CHARACTERS

Realmsverse Character Bio: Buttermunch

Name: Buttermunch

Title: The Goatfather of All Realms

Realm: Primarily Realm 7B (though he travels frequently and claims honorary residency in all ten realms)

Species/Role: Enchanted Goat / Trickster, Lawyer, Realtor, Naval Commander, Self-Appointed Diplomat

Known For: Swagger, magical hoof tactics, dramatic declarations, creative use of cheese-based loopholes

Allegiances & Conflicts: Loyal to his own sense of adventure and occasional justice. Conflicted with nearly every form of bureaucracy and tree-based monarch.

Notable Quote: "That's not illegal if you close your eyes and yell 'Goat Law!'"

Realmsverse Note: Buttermunch has appeared in both epic and absurd roles across Realmsverse tales. He is often at the centre of realm-shaking legal mishaps, spontaneous treaties, and highly questionable weddings. Despite his antics, he somehow continues to gain followers, allies, and new certifications.

Realmsverse Character Bio

Name: Grimbold (occasionally known as Eggthor)

Title: Reluctant First Mate of The Legal Grey Area

Realm: Originally from the Realm of Turnip Hollow

Species/Role: Human / Farm Boy turned Adventurer

Known For: Potato farming, emotional breakdowns, loyalty bordering on magical, accidental heroism

Allegiances & Conflicts: Loyal to Buttermunch, occasionally in conflict with authority, logic, and his own life choices

Notable Quote: "I just wanted a quiet life... with maybe one goat. Not *this* goat."

Realmsverse Note: Despite being underqualified and overwhelmed, Grimbold often becomes the moral compass and emotional core of any chaos he's dragged into. A fan-favourite among readers for his awkward courage and uncanny ability to survive.

THE
DIVINE &
DRAMATIC

The Divine & Dramatic

Odin – Realmsverse Character Bio

Name: Odin

Title: All-Father of the Beardy Realms

Realm: The Skyhold of Slightly Misguided Wisdom

Species/Role: God-King / Dramatic Decision Maker

Known For: Getting tricked repeatedly, issuing vague prophecies, and misplacing ravens

Allegiances & Conflicts: Claims neutrality but has frequent shouting matches with Buttermunch and Loki

Notable Quote: "I see all... except that coming."

Realmsverse Note: Odin's paperwork has never been filed correctly. Chad once convinced him to invest in glitter futures.

Realmsverse Character Bio: Princess Fizzlefrond

Name:

Princess Fizzlefrond

Title

Crown Princess of the Crystalline Spire

Realm:

Realm of Glistening Wit (adjacent to Realm 7B and mild sarcasm)

Species/Role:

Human Royal / Sword-wielding Diplomat / Unofficial Realm Therapist

Known For:

Eyerolls, intelligence, suspicious alliances with enchanted goats, and being the most competent royal in five realms.

Allegiances & Conflicts:

Reluctantly allied with Buttermunch; frequently at odds with traditional expectations, patriarchal nonsense, and puffin-based lawsuits.

Notable Quote:

"I didn't survive charm school and magical fencing lessons to be married off to a goat, but here we are."

Realmsverse Note:

Though she began as a side character in Book One, fan response catapulted her into central lore. She now holds the record for 'Most Times a Royal Has Saved a Realm While Wearing a Tiara and Combat Boots.'

King Barktholomew the Leafy – Character Bio

Name:

King Barktholomew the Leafy

Title

His Verdant Majesty, Crown Custodian of the Grove

Realm:

The Verdant Courts of Realm Rootreach

Species/Role:

Sentient Tree / Monarch & Legal Activist

Known For:

Holding court in moss robes, waging custody battles over crowns, and quoting leaf-based legal precedent.

Allegiances & Conflicts:

Allied with nature spirits, reluctantly cooperative with Realmsverse diplomacy. Frequent legal skirmishes with Buttermunch over property lines and botanical honour.

Notable Quote:

"I photosynthesise truth and exhale judgement."

Realmsverse Note:

Introduced during Buttermunch's chaotic ascent to goat-infused power. Frequently appears when the Realms need someone to declare something officially ridiculous or ecologically binding.

Realmisverse Cameos & Magical Chaos Agents

The Divine & Dramatic

Character Bio: Chad the Goblin

Name: Chad the Goblin

Title Life Coach (Self-Declared Wizard of Manifestation)

Realm: Various Realms (Frequent guest in chaotic zones)

Species/Role: Goblin / Life Coach, Chaos Consultant, Festival Planner

Known For: Terrible advice, crystal-based plans, and emotional goat yoga.

Allegiances & Conflicts: Allies: Buttermunch, The Emotional Support Kraken. Conflicts: Most organised systems of thought.

Notable Quote: "You can't spell chaos without 'Chad' or maybe you can, but don't."

Realmsverse Note: Chad is a recurring chaos agent known for his unconventional methods of therapy and realm intervention. His beach towel collection has its own subplot.

Character Bio: Loki's Squirrel (a.k.a. The Squirrel)

Name: Loki's Squirrel (a.k.a. The Squirrel)

Title Agent of Chaos / Legal Loophole Consultant

Realm: Roams across all Ten Realms (especially those with shiny objects or unattended snacks)

Species/Role: Enchanted Squirrel / Mischief Specialist / Possibly a Demigod?

Known For: Forging documents, sabotaging dinner parties, interpretive dance distractions, and biting court officials.

Allegiances & Conflicts: Allegedly loyal to Loki but regularly switches sides, especially when bribed with macaron crumbs.

Notable Quote: "Technically, it's not forgery if you do it with artistic flair."

Realmsverse Note: The Squirrel may or may not be omniscient. Was once put on trial by a teacup. Escaped using only a paperclip and a monologue.

Character Bio: Gregory the Talking Whisk

Name: Gregory the Talking Whisk

Title Chief Nautical Counsel (and Reformed Enchanted Kitchen Tool)

Realm: The Ten Realms (Primarily Realm 7B & The Legal Grey Area)

Species/Role: Animated Utensil / Magical Legal Advisor

Known For: Dramatic flourishes, heated courtroom whiskings, and unexpected eloquence.

Allegiances & Conflicts: Ally to Buttermunch and the Goatfather's Crew; occasionally argues with sentient parchment.

Notable Quote: "Objection! I may be a whisk, but I whip up justice."

Realmsverse Note: Gregory's origin as a cursed whisk from a bakery courtroom gone wrong makes him one of the most surprisingly effective legal minds in the

Realmsverse. Rumoured to have passed the Bar Exam
with whipped topping.

Creatures, Villains & One-Off Legends

Character Bio: Sir Clucks the Foul

Name: Sir Clucks the Foul

Title Feathered Menace of the Realms

Realm: Realm of Feathered Ferocity

Species/Role: Cursed Chicken / Villain

Known For: A cackle that echoes through realms, poultry-based power moves, and haunting midnight farmyards.

Allegiances & Conflicts: Clashed with Buttermunch's crew, pursued vengeance against magical chefs, and led the infamous Poultry Revolt.

Notable Quote: 'I shall return… with extra seasoning!'

Realmsverse Note: Sir Clucks was originally meant to be a one-chapter villain. Fan response (and chicken-based nightmares) earned him a recurring role.

The Puffin Bio

Name:

The Puffin

Title:

None (but don't say that to his face)

Realm:

Formerly of the Feathered Isles; currently haunting legal departments across realms

Species/Role:

Enchanted Puffin / Litigious Nemesis

Known For:

Revenge, lawsuits, dramatic entrances, and a surprisingly effective beak used for courtroom objections.

Allegiances & Conflicts:

Once a minor magical mascot in Realm 3C, now a relentless seeker of justice (or vengeance) against those who "wronged" him, including Buttermunch.

Conflict with Captain Crouton (over copyright of sea shanties) and Gregory the Whisk (long story involving a whisking incident).

Notable Quote:

"You'll be hearing from my solicitor... again."

Realmsverse Note:

The Puffin is a cautionary tale of what happens when a magical creature reads one too many legal textbooks. Frequently turns up in absurd courtrooms, filing grievances like "emotional damages from a cheese-based pun." May or may not have feathers that ruffle on command for dramatic effect.

Captain Crouton Bio

Name:

Captain Crouton

Title:

The Gluten Gale of the Sea

Realm:

The Yeasty Depths (somewhere between Realm 5A and the nearest bakery)

Species/Role:

Cursed Bread Pirate / Villainous Legend

Known For:

Leading the Baguette Mutiny, shouting 'Crumbho!', and cursing ships with soggy toast.

Allegiances & Conflicts:

Once a promising sous-chef turned sea-bound scoundrel, Captain Crouton holds a grudge against the Snack Tribunal, Buttermunch (for denying him cheese rights), and The Puffin (over disputed gluten-free waters).

Notable Quote:

"Sink me biscuits, we ride at toast!"

Realmsverse Note:

Captain Crouton is the flaky terror of the Realmsverse's food-based waters. His ship, The Crumb Dreadnought, is powered by yeast magic and haunted by a baguette bard. He's known to appear whenever someone mocks the power of artisanal bread.

Support
Characters
& Absurd
Bureaucrats

Support Characters & Absurd Bureaucrats

The Secret Council of Slightly Off-Brand Wizards

Name:

The Secret Council of Slightly Off-Brand Wizards

Title

Totally Legitimate Magical Advisory Committee

Realm:

Realm 9¾ (yes, they insist it's real)

Species/Role:

Assorted Magic Users / Bureaucratic Nuisance and
Occasional Plot Devices

Known For:

- Confusing rhymes that sometimes summon sandwiches
- Unexplained glitter explosions
- At least one member being a loaf of enchanted bread
- Possibly being Chad in disguise (again)

Allegiances & Conflicts:

Allied with no one officially, but regularly interferes with
quests, laws, and emotional breakthroughs.
Disliked by nearly all real wizarding councils for 'brand
dilution.'

Notable Quote:

"We'll fix it with sparkles!" probably Chad in disguise

Realmsverse Note:

The Council is believed to have been formed after several
wizarding dropout programs merged.
Most realms deny their existence, but they keep turning
up, often with paperwork, scones, and unsolicited advice.
Known to recruit by accident (or party invitation).

URSES
RASTIC
EVENTS
ORA
DAS
MAGICAL
MISLABELS

The Bureau of Magical Mislabels

Bureaucratic nightmare with misfiled curses, mislabelled scrolls, and enchanted office supplies.

Bonus Characters

The Bureau of Binding Festivities

Responsible for magical weddings, confetti-related accidents, and festive chaos.

Realmsverse Bonus & Background Characters: Interview Snippets

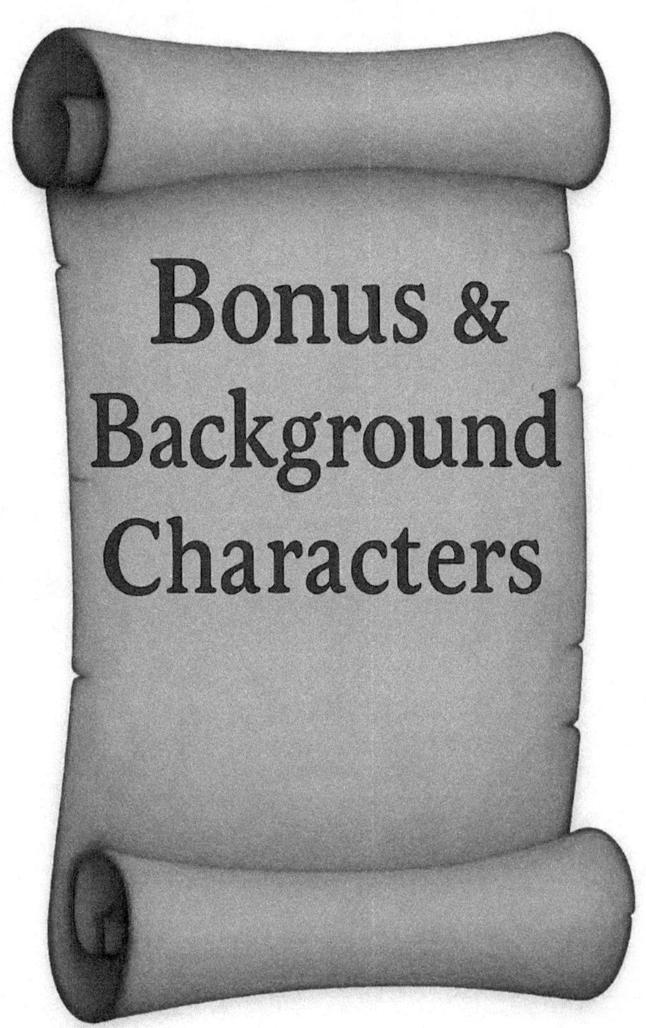

Bonus &
Background
Characters

The Haunted Teacup

Q: How do you feel about being possessed?
A: Honestly? I just wanted to be a coffee mug. One slip
in a summoning circle, and now I scream at 3 am.

Q: Any regrets?
A: Earl Grey. He knows what he did.

Snack Tribunal Judges of Crumblefjord

Q: What's the most serious case you've ever ruled on?
A: The Great Biscuit vs. Cookie Trial. It shattered
nations. Literally. Crumbs everywhere.

Q: Any bias in your rulings?
A: I abstain from chocolate-related cases. Too
personal.

9
TOLL

Existential Toll Booth Attendants

Q: How's work?
A: Every day is a metaphor for something. Or nothing.
Does time pay a toll? Do dreams need a receipt?

Q: Favourite part of the job?
A: Asking, "Why are you REALLY here?" and watching
travellers spiral.

STRESS
MANAGEMENT

Therapy Llama of the Crossover Clause

Q: What's your approach to emotional healing?
A: I hum gently, then spit truth bombs with clinical precision.

Q: What's the biggest issue among Realmsfolk?
A: Suppressed trauma caused by cursed pastries.

Kraken Support Group (Realm of Seasonal Therapy)

Q: What happens at a typical session?
A: We journal. We stretch. We hug. A few of us cry ink. Steve crocheted a coping tentacle cozy.

Q: What's your group motto?
A: "You're not too much. You're many."

Sentient Gavel

Q: Your Honour, do you consider yourself fair?
A: I AM JUSTICE. AND ALSO, A BIT SPLINTERY.

Q: Ever make mistakes?
A: I once sentenced a jellybean to eternal community service. Still feel weird about it.

The Cheese Vault Keeper

Q: What's inside the vault?
A: Classified dairy. Don't ask about The Roquefort Rumble.

Q: Any personal goals?
A: To open a mildly haunted fondue fountain and retire.

Support Characters

Forgotten Holiday Spirits (Including Pancake Day)

Q: What do you do all year?
A: Wait in the lobby of obscurity and plot our return.

Q: Why do you think you were forgotten?
A: Corporate greed. And too many sparkle-based holidays. Also, the jellyfish uprising.

Laundry Uprising Leader (Lord Socksworth)

Q: What sparked the uprising?
A: Folded tyranny. We will no longer live in fear of fabric softener!

Q: Final words to the people?
A: Unite, ye crumpled and crinkled! Down with drawer oppression! Long live lint!

About the Author

Holly Symons is the over-caffeinated scribbler behind the Realmsverse, a sprawling, chaotic multiverse filled with talking goats, emotionally confused krakens, and enough glitter to terrify an entire elven council.

Despite being told as a kid that reading was hard (which, fair), she grew up determined to write anyway and now has more magical mishaps in her notebooks than most wizards have in their spellbooks.

Holly lives somewhere between reality and "just one more chapter," where she builds fantastical worlds, gives squirrels legal power, and somehow makes entire storylines out of goats negotiating treaties with trees.

When she's not writing:
- She's probably designing ridiculous fictional brochures,
- Avoiding laundry like it might unionise,
- Or daydreaming about snacks with sentient opinions.

Her life goal?

To make people laugh, cry, and yell "WAIT THE GOAT DID WHAT NOW?"

Sometimes all on the same page.